KAIGHLA RISES

Ask the Waves Why

A Novel

Copyright © 2024 by Kaighla Rises

All rights reserved. No part of this publication may be reproduced, stored or transmitted in any form or by any means, electronic, mechanical, photocopying, recording, scanning, or otherwise without written permission from the publisher. It is illegal to copy this book, post it to a website, or distribute it by any other means without permission.

This novel is entirely a work of fiction. The names, characters and incidents portrayed in it are the work of the author's imagination. Any resemblance to actual persons, living or dead, events or localities is entirely coincidental.

First edition

ISBN: 979-8-218-33467-3

This book was professionally typeset on Reedsy. Find out more at reedsy.com

"Strictly speaking, all our memories
are lies we tell ourselves."

DANIEL NAYERI

I

Part One

Chapter 1

Twenty minutes before the phone rings, Caroline Rush is reading in her favorite chair, basking in the amber glow of autumn sunlight filtering through the half-drawn blinds. Behind her, Lake Michigan shimmers under a veil of morning mist.

A bottle of wine stands empty on the dining room table alongside two crystal glasses—a testament to last night's reveries. One glass lies on its side with a line of syrupy-sweet red dripping out of it, down the side of the table, pooling on the herringbone floor.

As she reads, Caroline is unaware of the bombshell that's about to upend her life yet again—oblivious to everything other than the lyrical prose on the page. She's *content* for the first time in years. Not happy, necessarily—that would be too much to ask. But she's found a semblance of peace.

A garbage truck rumbles down the road in front of her cabin, bringing her back to reality. Caroline sighs and closes the book she's been reading, setting it on the table next to her chair. She takes a sip of her coffee—sweet, no cream, lukewarm now.

As she stands to refill her mug with fresh coffee from the carafe, she stumbles against the footstool, cursing under her breath. One would think she'd move the chair, but that spot has the best lighting in the house, perfect for reading, so she leaves it and endures the bruised toes.

She climbed out of bed at 7 a.m. this morning, like she does almost every morning—most days greeted by Netflix's annoying "Are you *still* watching?" screen on her laptop. But not this morning. No, today there was a gloriously hung Italian man, half her age, spooning her naked ass when she opened her eyes.

Luciano is still snoring away in the bedroom when her phone rings, a call from a number she doesn't recognize. She's in no mood to talk to anyone this early on a Saturday morning, let alone someone from *that* area code, so she sends it to voicemail. They call back, though, twice more. So, she puts her slippers on and throws Luciano's wool coat over her nightgown. She grabs a lighter and a cigarette from the pack in the cabinet and steps outside onto the deck, slipping the sliding door shut behind her as she dials the number.

"Hello?" the voice on the other end says.

She knows that voice. She *loves* that voice. She *hates* that voice.

"Don't hang up. Please," he says.

Caroline lights up her cigarette and takes a long drag. "Fine," she says, her heart racing. "You've got two minutes."

"I need to talk to you," he says.

"So talk."

"No, not like this, not over the phone."

"Look," Caroline says, taking another drag on the cigarette and picking a tobacco flake off her lip. "I'm not going through

CHAPTER 1

this with you, not again."

"No, no. It's nothing like that. I just... this is something we should discuss face-to-face." There's an ambulance flying past him, among other city noises in the background. "I'm in Chicago for a conference and I have some free time tomorrow evening. Meet me?"

Caroline shakes her head, like it's an Etch-a-Sketch she can shake to clear out the memories. "I hate when you do this to me," she says, wiping last night's mascara from under her eyes. Out of the corner of her eye, she sees Luciano standing in the kitchen, naked as the day he was born, his messy black hair dancing around his ears as he stretches.

"It won't take long. Please just come, Lina," the man on the phone says, snapping her back to the moment.

Lina. The sound of that name in his mouth sends chills down her spine. It's been so long since anyone called her that.

"Fine. Where?" she asks. Her stomach is already twisting with anxiety and anticipatory regret.

"That Lebanese restaurant, the one close to Lincoln Park. Say around four o'clock tomorrow?" he asks.

Luciano taps on the window to get Caroline's attention. He mimics holding a phone and cocks his head to the side as if to ask who she's talking to. When she grimaces, he nods in acknowledgment and frowns, then dons an apron to get started on breakfast—*only* an apron. *Sweet Jesus.*

"Fine. See you then," she says, ending the call and taking another long drag on her cigarette.

She stands on the deck for a few moments, watching as a family walks along the lake shore. The children are running ahead as their parents chase after them with a trained eye.

The faces of Caroline's own children flash through her mind, suspended in time at the ages she remembers them best—all those years ago, before her life imploded, leaving her drowning in an ocean of wine and self-loathing.

After one last hit on her cigarette, she drops it on the deck, grinds it down with her slipper, and steps into the cabin, shivering as her body adjusts to the warmth.

"So, him again?" Luciano asks as he kisses her on the cheek.

"Yep," Caroline says, coughing as she blows on her hands to warm them.

"I thought he didn't have your new number?" he asks, handing her a plate of bacon and eggs.

"The internet is a magical place," she says, taking a seat on the stool next to the island. That's the only way he could have gotten her number, after all. No one would have given it to him, not after everything he's put her through.

"What did he want this time?" Luciano asks as he stands wiping the cast-iron pan clean before hanging it on the hook above the island.

"Nothing important," she says, avoiding eye contact. Luciano is her hard-earned reward—her reprieve, her luxury cruise after decades of hell. Why complicate things?

"Hmm. Well, let's forget about it then. Eat your eggs, *amore*," he says, kissing her cheek and sitting next to her to eat his breakfast.

Caroline smiles and takes a few bites, willing herself to focus on the moment. But her mind keeps replaying the memory of the last time she saw the man on the phone. Before she knows it, she's finished her plate and Luciano is washing dishes.

"What are you up to today?" she asks as she gets busy cleaning up the wine mess from yesterday.

"I need to head back to Milwaukee to prepare for that

CHAPTER 1

meeting on Monday. If I leave things to Carl, we'll never sign another client," he says, pulling off the rubber gloves and draping them across the lip of the sink. "But I thought I'd lounge here with you a bit longer. You're not gonna throw me out just yet, are you?" he asks, smiling flirtatiously and pulling her closer to him.

Caroline's chest is tight. She feels that old familiar urge to close the doors on everyone and go inward, to focus on the fire burning inside—the fire that will die out if she doesn't keep it hot with focused, bitter rage. The fire that protects her from the ocean of sorrow waiting to take her down again.

But a more primal urge takes over. So she lets him carry her to bed and have his way with her, reminding her of one of the many reasons she's sleeping with a man half her age.

They spend the rest of the day snuggling and snacking on fruit and cheese and watching mind-numbing reality TV. Just what the doctor ordered.

* * *

It's raining as Luciano drives away from her cabin later that evening. She relaxes on the sofa with the book she started in the morning but finds herself unable to focus for more than a few seconds. She can't stop thinking about seeing him tomorrow, about what he wants to talk about—if it's actually a conversation he wants with her and not something more.

She gives up on the book and opens a bottle of wine, wrapping herself in a blanket and turning on a movie she's watched a dozen times. She falls asleep right there on the sofa.

Chapter 2

Caroline is jolted awake by the sound of the doorbell ringing. She sits up and rubs her eyes, opening them one at a time against the sun's dazzling reflection on the lake. The ringing persists, repeating every few seconds.

"Yeah, I hear you!" she yells from the sofa, searching for her slippers.

Just then, Mimi flutters past her toward the front door. "Thanks, but no thanks. In this house, we revere the old gods!" With that, she closes the door in their face. "Yeah, Tink! Sic 'em!" she says, egging on her yipping Yorkie.

Caroline stumbles off the sofa in time to see two men hurrying down the driveway. They're dressed in their Sunday best, carrying pamphlets.

"Not even God rests on the Sabbath anymore," Mimi quips.

"Oh no. Don't make me laugh!" Caroline whines, holding her head and pointing at the aspirin on the upper shelf. "I hope you paid Tinkerbell's trainer what he's worth. She's awful good at keeping quiet when you break into people's houses," Caroline says, accepting two aspirin and a glass of water from Mimi.

CHAPTER 2

"It's not *breaking in* if you gave me the key," Mimi retorts. She sits at the table and takes a drink of Caroline's tepid coffee from the day before. She frowns and places the mug in the microwave. "And at least I didn't show up Friday night when Luke was here. Not even Tink could muffle the volume of noise you two make in the sack."

Caroline throws a pillow at Mimi, narrowly missing her head.

"Hey! Foul!" Mimi laughs before coming to sit on the sofa next to Caroline, mug in hand.

"I didn't even know you were in town," Caroline says, pulling her little sister in for a sideways hug.

Mimi shrugs. "I have a consultation with an artist in Racine tomorrow morning, so I thought I'd crash at your place. Better than spending a shit-ton on an overpriced Airbnb owned by some twat in Seattle or something."

The hours tick by as the two of them catch up, picking up where they left off the last time Mimi dropped in—like no time had passed at all. Mimi tells Caroline all about her new art studio in Chicago and the various men she's been entertaining. Caroline tells Mimi about the screenplay she's working on these days. Mimi wants to know how things are going with Luciano, now that he and Caroline have been together for a year.

Caroline remembers him standing naked in the kitchen in all his glory yesterday morning and feels a slight tug in her womb, as she always does when she thinks of him naked. Memories of their afternoon together dance across her vision, momentarily taking her out of the current moment. And then she remembers the phone call.

Shit, the meeting! she thinks, noting the time and mentally calculating how long it will take to make the drive to Chicago.

"So how long are you staying?" she asks Mimi as she pours herself a fresh cup of coffee and tries to seem casual.

"Why? You got more plans with Luke? Or some other poor schmuck? You holding out on me?!" Mimi asks.

"Me? *Never*," Caroline smirks. "I just have somewhere to be. You don't mind, do you?" she asks as she heads to the bathroom for a quick shower.

"Do I mind having this whole place to myself? Ha!" Mimi laughs, grabbing the remote from the coffee table. She flips on the TV and scrolls through Caroline's recently viewed Netflix shows. "*Godddd* why do you suck so hard?" Mimi scoffs. "Outlander?! *Really?*"

"Hey, that show is the shit!" Caroline yells from the bathroom as she turns on the water and grabs a towel from the linen closet.

"Mm-hmm. Sure it is!" Mimi yells back.

After her shower, Caroline dresses and grabs a bag from the bottom of her closet, slipping a change of clothes inside. She applies her favorite perfume—a dab behind each earlobe and one on each wrist, rubbing them together to spread the scent. After drying her graying blonde curls, she pulls her hair back, securing it with a claw clip.

As she sits in front of the vanity mirror in her room and applies some mascara—waterproof, just in case—she pauses for a moment, looking into her blue eyes, then quickly looks away. The last thing she wants to do is give herself enough time to think through what she's about to do. She tosses the mascara in her bag, along with the perfume and her toothbrush.

Caroline heads to the entryway, dropping her bag by the

CHAPTER 2

front door. She knows she should say goodbye to Mimi, but hesitates, unsure how to dodge her questions. But there's no need.

"You forgot your phone," Mimi says, eyeing it on the coffee table. Her tone has taken on a noticeably more serious quality in the last fifteen minutes.

Caroline picks up the phone. There's a new message notification on the screen. It's from him, asking if she's on the road yet and wishing her a safe drive.

"What's his excuse this time?" Mimi asks, rubbing Tink's head without looking away from the TV screen.

"Michelle, come on. Please. I can't fight with you about this right now. It's not like before. I just need to talk to him. Or... *he* needs to talk to *me* about something, and I need to know what's going on. I promise we can talk about it when I get back, okay?"

Mimi stands and approaches Caroline, looking disappointed. Caroline could never handle that look. "You can use my government name all you want and I still won't side with you on this," Mimi replies. "But there's no sense in beating a dead horse. Just... do me a solid and come home in one piece, okay?"

"I'll be fine," Caroline says, jangling her keys nervously. Mimi isn't often serious, but when she is, she means it. "You'll be okay here, right? Do you need some money for takeout?"

"Nope. We're good," she says. "But hey I call dibs on this place if you die. I'll shank Audrey for it. Don't think I won't!" With that, she stands and heads to the kitchen, hunting around the fridge for a snack.

"Okay byeee," Caroline says, drawing the word out like the two of them always do, and shuts the door behind her.

Once in the car, Caroline shoots him a text to say she's headed that way. He doesn't respond right away, making her even more anxious.

You're not actually looking forward to this?! Caroline scolds herself. *Not him, not now. Not after everything that's happened.* But alone in the car, with miles of reception-less pavement ahead of her, without even a podcast or audiobook to distract her from her thoughts, they're all about him.

He replies ten minutes into the drive, confirming he'll see her soon. The butterflies in her stomach when she sees his message confirm she is *definitely* looking forward to this.

Chapter 3

The air is thick with hookah smoke and the bitter smell of Turkish coffee overflowing and burning on the stovetop. Everywhere, from floor to ceiling, is covered in rich, honey-brown wood. They claim it's Lebanese cedar, and who can argue?

He's taken the seat facing the wall, which isn't like him. But then, it's been years since she last saw him, and Lord knows she's changed, so he surely has, too.

Several men are sitting on cushions against the wall, sharing a hookah and throwing back drinks. They're staring at her as she walks toward the booth, making comments about her body in Arabic.

The sound of the men laughing and heckling one another makes him turn to see what all the fuss is about. The moment his eyes lock with Caroline's, the snake of anxiety in her belly coils tighter.

There he is—Hassan, *her Hassan*. His face is creased with the beginnings of wrinkles and his short, coarse black hair and beard are peppered with white. For a split second, her mind wanders back to the last time she had a handful of his hair in her fist, but she catches herself.

He stands and gestures to the opposite bench, inviting her to sit. "Sorry about that. You know how young men can be..."

"Don't apologize for them. You don't even know them," Caroline replies, smiling, but keeping her eyes down.

"*Alhamdulillah,* you've arrived safely. Any trouble on the road?" he asks.

"None," she says, trying to act normal, like her insides aren't screaming to either kiss him or leave now and be done with it forever.

Mercifully, the server comes to take their orders and brings a couple of glasses of water, breaking up the tension.

"*Shoukran,*" Hassan says, thanking him. "Let's have some *kahwa* and iced water... how about some falafel and hummus to start," he says. "Make sure it's fresh, eh, Mo? None of that stuff from last night." The two men carry on in Arabic for a few minutes like the best of friends.

A few minutes later, Mo brings Caroline's glass of iced water and Hassan's Turkish coffee out. There's steam pouring from the top of the tiny ceramic cup.

They dance around the elephant in the room for several more minutes while Caroline struggles to maintain her composure. Hassan is going on and on about something at work when she can't take it anymore.

"Look, that's interesting. Really," she says, cutting him off. "But can we cut the small talk?" she asks, just as Mo brings the falafel and hummus over.

Hassan thanks Mo and takes a sip of his Turkish coffee—still too hot. He sits looking at the wall behind her, then down at his hands, then directly into her eyes. "You look well, Lina," he

CHAPTER 3

says, moving his hands closer to hers on the table.

"Why do you insist on calling me that?" she asks, taking a drink of water to disguise her voice cracking.

"Old habits," he says and moves his hands back to his lap.

"Is it your dad? *What's going on?*"

He smiles. "Baba's fine. Thank you for asking."

"That's good to hear," Caroline says. "So, what it is?"

Hassan takes another sip of coffee. "First, I need you to know that I love you. That hasn't changed," he says.

This is the moment Caroline will remember years from now when she mulls over what came next—him telling her that he loves her, unbid, before dropping an atomic bomb on her heart.

"You're the mother of my children. We're *family*, forever," he continues.

Tears are burning in the corners of Caroline's eyes. "That's very nice to hear," she says, setting her glass down. "But I wish you would just spill it. Honestly, Hassan, it takes you ten years to get to the p—"

"I've met someone," he says, cutting her off. "It's pretty serious."

Caroline takes a deep breath to steady herself. "And?"

"And I thought you should hear it from me."

"You're free to do as you like, Hassan," Caroline says. "It's none of my business. But I don't understand why you felt like this was something you needed to tell me *in person*. Just couldn't resist the urge to watch me fall apart, huh? Why are you so *cruel*?"

Hassan drops his chin to his chest. "I thought it was the most respectful way to tell you," he says, his voice cracking. "And please, let's not hurt one another, okay? Haven't we *both* had enough hurt?"

"Stop," Caroline says, holding up her hand and choking back sobs. *"You* don't get to talk to *me* about hurt, not after—"

"Let's get out of here," Hassan says, throwing some cash on the table and standing to leave.

* * *

An hour later, they're standing in Hassan's hotel room. He's helping Caroline out of her coat, then closing the curtains, then pouring her a glass of water.

Caroline doesn't remember deciding to climb into his car. She doesn't recall agreeing to ride with him to his hotel or walking into the elevator with him. Her body simply took over and she followed him, leaving her mind and heart behind. She would have to deal with them later, she knew. And Luciano—him, too.

She cringes knowing how disappointed he would be if he knew where she is and with whom. Not so much because of the infidelity—that he could forgive, she hopes—but for betraying herself like this, and with *him* of all people.

Hassan takes her hand in his, running his finger along the lines of her palm. "I've memorized these hands," he says, lifting his eyes to meet her gaze. "And those eyes."

Caroline stands frozen in place, in time, feeling the familiar sensation of Hassan's energy flooding her own, washing through her veins like a virus seeking to devour every healthy cell it encounters.

"Hassan," she mumbles as he pulls her closer. "You said you met someone…"

CHAPTER 3

"*Shhh,*" Hassan says, lifting her blouse over her head. "There's no one here but me and you. Just you and me, Lina. No one else matters." He leads her to the bathroom, turns on the shower, helps her inside, and steps in to join her. Caroline focuses on the feeling of the scalding water on her skin, the smell of the expensive hotel soap as he lathers her up.

After the shower, they dry off and lay in bed, saying nothing for a long time, gazing into one another's eyes.

Hassan kisses her sweetly. "Lina," he whispers, brushing a knuckle along her jaw. "My *Lina.*"

There's no turning back now. Like an addict finally getting a hit after years of going without, Caroline dives into him. Soon, she will be just another part of him, a colonized land he claimed decades ago and left in ruins but maintains an iron grip over.

She's kissing him harder now, unable to slow herself. It's like riding a bicycle—no matter how many years pass between these meetings, they never forget the steps. He knows all the secret places she likes to be kissed and massaged and licked. She climaxes hard, crying and laughing and moaning, equal parts euphoric and bereft.

Hassan takes his time reaching his own climax. He wants her to *enjoy it*. He enters her, paying careful attention to the way she moves, adjusting the depth and speed of his thrusts in response. He's gentle with her, tender even. Because she's the mother of his children, after all, and she deserves some goddamned tenderness.

Caroline moans in ecstasy as he wraps his hands around her throat and thrusts harder and deeper. When he finishes, he collapses onto her, breathing in the smell of her hair and kissing her.

Their clock has begun to tick down; He will be gone soon. So she pulls him in close, begging all the gods to let her die next to him that night. Because death is better than facing herself in the harsh light of morning.

Chapter 4

SEVENTEEN YEARS AGO

He wasn't breathing. Caroline was sure of it.

"Babe, I'm heading out," she said, nudging him. He didn't flinch. "Mark, come, *on*," she said, pushing her hair out of her face and sighing in frustration. "You gotta stop doing this shit."

He'd started drinking at 11 a.m., as he often did. Now, as the sun was setting behind the mountains, he lay unconscious on the duvet with drool dripping from the corner of his mouth.

Just as she was about to call 911, Mark started coughing.

"Oh, thank God!" she exclaimed, helping him sit up.

He opened his mouth to say something before his face turned various shades of green. Caroline handed him the wastebasket just in time, then ran to grab a hand towel from the adjacent bathroom. She ran it under warm water and came back into his bedroom to clean his face.

"Baby, I love you so much," he mumbled, grabbing her hand as she stood to leave.

"Mm-hmm, you too. Sleep well," she said, pulling her hand free just before he passed out again.

It had been eleven years since she'd moved to L.A. with Paul, her high school sweetheart. They'd headed out west on a whim when she was heavily pregnant with Audrey. They weren't sure what was awaiting them there, but they knew it *had* to be better than rural Indiana.

A year after they moved into their tiny apartment in West Hollywood, two police officers showed up on her doorstep on a nondescript Thursday evening. Paul had been killed in a motorcycle accident on the freeway on his way home from work.

At just twenty years old with a new baby, Caroline had to figure out how to navigate life in Los Angeles. Though her dad and Mimi begged her to come back home, Caroline insisted on staying. Sure, it was hard, but L.A. offered her and Audrey more opportunities, and Caroline thought maybe she could make good on her promise to herself to give screenwriting a try. Plus, she hoped she may one day meet a man half as interesting and warm as Paul had been.

Caroline had found to her dismay that the only thing *less* abundant in L.A. than well-paying writing gigs was men with any actual substance. She'd dated all sorts—bankers and actors and hedge-fund managers and teachers and backup dancers—and she hadn't been able to tolerate any of them longer than a few months.

She wanted so much for Audrey to have a normal life, a *stable* life, but no matter how hard she worked, it felt like there

CHAPTER 4

was no hope of providing either stability or normalcy without a man by her side—a man with money, preferably. It was well and good to be a strong, independent woman, but in *this economy...*

So try as she may to take things slow, she'd invariably invite them to move in by month four, and the relationship would fizzle out not much later.

Then, she'd met Mark at a Lakers game. He was there with a guy her friend Maria was dating, and he'd been kind and funny. He wasn't the sharpest pencil in the box, but Audrey had approved of him and Caroline couldn't find a good excuse to end it, so they'd been dating for nearly a year. Somehow, she'd managed to break her cycle and avoid moving him in.

But things had been cooling off between the two of them for weeks, and Caroline couldn't put her finger on why. Not that she needed to look far for reasons. Aside from his binge drinking, which had always bothered her, they had nothing whatsoever in common. So she started looking for her exit.

Mark was snoring loudly.

Well, at least I know he's alive, Caroline thought as she slipped her heels back on, grabbed her cardigan, and closed the door behind her. As she turned to walk back into the fray, she slammed right into someone's face.

"Oh, I'm sorry!" she exclaimed.

"No, it's my fault. I wasn't looking," the stranger offered, holding his nose.

"Oh, God. I... are you bleeding? Should I find you a towel?"

"No, I'm good. Just a bump. No harm done."

Caroline fumbled for the hall light switch and flipped it, giving her a better look at him. He was about her height, wearing dark denim jeans and a tight-fitted black t-shirt. His dark hair was cropped on the sides, and his eyes were sharp, wise, and dark as midnight. His smile was warm, and he had a jawline that could cut through solid rock. He smelled so good she could barely stand it. That's when it dawned on Caroline that she'd seen him before.

"Wait, I think I know you," he said, taking the words out of her mouth.

"Yeah, I was just thinking the same thing," she said.

He stood pondering for a minute. "Oh! That coffee shop in Glendale, right? At the corner of Glenoaks & Western? Was that you slinging espresso shots the other day? Or... attempting to, before your little accident?" he asked, chuckling.

"Yep, that was me," Caroline admitted, blushing. "In my defense, I'm not usually so clumsy. That was a rough shift."

"I knew it! I never forget a face," he said. "And hey, we've all been there. I'm sure you're much more competent usually."

Caroline smirked. "Yeah, I do my best. It's just my part-time gig. Brings in a little more reliable money than screenwriting these days," she said, trying not to make it too obvious how desperately broke she was.

"Are you new to the area? I haven't seen you there before," he asked. "I live not far from there, up in La Cañada."

"Not new, no. But I just transferred to that location from Pasadena."

"Ah, that explains it."

"Do you usually keep such close track of your baristas?"

"Like I said, I would have remembered you," he said, flirting with his midnight eyes.

Caroline stared at the ground awkwardly, transferring her weight from leg to leg. "So... do you come out to the valley

CHAPTER 4

often?" she asked, trying to break the silence.

"Sure do. Looking for beautiful women like you, of course."

"Ha! Well, they're downstairs and probably pretty drunk by now. You'd better hurry before some other guy snatches them up."

"Nah, I'm just kidding," he said, laughing. "That's not really my thing."

"Oh? Not into philandering? I hear it's all the rage these days."

"Not for me, not anymore. I'm a *reformed* philanderer."

"How unfortunate. You're still so young!"

"I'm not *that* young," he said. "Anyway, my cousin Ali dragged me out here to see Mark, but we can't seem to find him."

"Your cousin knows Mark?" Caroline asked. "Are they like… work buddies or something?"

"You could call it that. They *met* at work."

Caroline raised a quizzical brow. "Oh?"

"It didn't come from me, but they've been messing around for a few weeks. Ali won't shut up about him. It's getting pretty irritating."

And there it was—her explanation for the recent cool-off, as well as her excuse to finally end things with Mark. "I see. Well, he's passed out in his room if you wanna go tell her where to find him."

"Wait, tell who?" he asked.

"Your cousin…"

"Oh! No, Ali's… a *man*…"

Caroline's mouth fell open.

"I guess I don't have to ask how *you* know Mark, from that look on your face," he said, apologetically.

"Yeah…" she replied, throwing her cardigan on.

"Ali! Over here!" he said as a man walked toward them in the hall.

Caroline made her exit before things could get more awkward. But as she walked away, she realized she didn't know his name, and she *badly* wanted to know his name.

"Hey!" he called out from behind her. "Wait up!"

She stopped and turned toward him. "Yeah?"

"I'm glad I caught you before you left," he said, out of breath. "You wanna grab something to drink? Maybe take a walk?"

Caroline smiled, grateful for the offer of alcohol at that particular moment. "Well, I'd love that drink, but only if we can *please* not discuss this whole 'your-cousin-is-fucking-my-soon-to-be-ex-boyfriend' situation," she said, smiling awkwardly.

"Deal."

"Perfect. I'm Caroline, by the way."

"*Lina*," he said sweetly, smiling. "It's an Arabic name, but it fits you. Can I call you Lina?"

"Only if you tell me your name—the one your mother gave you, to be clear."

"Hassan. Hassan Mustafa Soliman," he replied, extending his hand to shake hers. "Shall we grab those drinks then, Lina?"

Chapter 5

They walked along the beach talking for hours that night, drinking and sharing stories and watching the waves roll in under the full moon. Eventually, they stopped walking and found a dry spot to sit on the warm sand.

"So tell me about your family," Caroline asked. She had told him about Mimi, about their strong and steady father, Charlie, about their mother's death when Caroline was seven years old, about growing up in Indiana. She was dying to know more about him.

"I'm not very close with my parents," Hassan said. "My father worked a lot, so he wasn't around much. I understand why now, but back then it was hard for me. I wanted to play soccer with him and see him at my school events, like all the other kids, but... well, he wanted us to have a better life than his childhood back home," he said, tossing a seashell down the beach. "He grew up really poor."

"Where is he from?" Caroline asked.

"A small town in Egypt, a few hours from Cairo. He immigrated to Kansas City in the late '80s. He married my mom and brought her over not long after. She spent most of my life kinda passing in and out since she went back and forth to visit her family in Egypt a lot."

"Egypt! How cool! Have you been to visit?"

"Oh, many times. My parents sent us to stay with my grandparents in the village every summer and winter break, so we could keep up a close relationship with our family there. They didn't want us to forget how to speak Arabic, too."

"I bet it was peaceful," Caroline remarked. "Life in their village, I mean."

"We didn't stay there the whole time. There was plenty of excitement, believe me!" he said, laughing. "That was the beginning of my philandering days, actually."

"Oh, do tell!"

So he told her all about how he and his brother and friends would spend their summers partying and trying to pick up older foreign women in resort cities like Sharm el-Sheikh and Hurghada. In the winter, they'd cruise around Cairo in his cousin's *tuk-tuk* looking for action, much to the chagrin of their relatives back in the village.

Caroline listened in rapture, trying to conjure a picture in her mind of the places he described. "I bet it was exciting to see the pyramids and the tombs of the Pharaohs and all that. I haven't traveled much," she said. "I mean, I spent a semester abroad in France during my senior year of high school, if that counts for anything."

"Of course, it counts," he replied.

"So what brought you to L.A.?" Caroline asked. "I mean aside from the ladies?"

"A lady, believe it or not," he said, kicking a rock on the sand.

"Now *there's* a story I wanna hear!" Caroline said, mimicking

CHAPTER 5

pulling out a pencil and pad of paper. "Tell me, did she break your heart? Or... no! She left you for another woman!"

Hassan laughed. "You certainly have an active imagination, I'll give you that!"

"I'm a writer. It's what we do," Caroline said.

"Well, I'm sorry to disappoint, but it wasn't nearly as exciting as all that," he said. "We just realized we'd grown apart. Or rather, we'd never grown close in the first place. Our parents set us up, and I moved out here to be closer to her. We gave it our best, but we just didn't have much in common."

"I see," Caroline said. "I'm sorry."

"Don't be," he said, smiling.

Talking with Hassan felt easy. He asked thoughtful questions and took a sincere interest in the answers, and his laugh was contagious. They discovered a shared love of old books and antiques and a mutual distaste for pickles and Diet Coke.

What she *didn't* tell him screamed in her mind. But experience had taught her that talking about one's child tended to kill the vibe, and this was a vibe she wanted to keep very much alive.

The more they talked, the better she felt, almost forgetting about the impending break-up conversation she'd have to have with Mark in the morning.

"It's getting pretty late," she said, realizing what time it was. "I'd better call a cab." The wine was getting to her. She worried she'd fall asleep right there on the sand.

"Do you live in Glendale? I could drop you off if you like. It's on the way," he offered.

"That's super kind of you," she replied. Maybe he was just trying to be polite.

"I insist," he smiled and stood, dusting his pants off and

reaching out a hand to help her up.

She knew it was probably a horrible idea to get into a car with this man, drunk as she was. But as she grabbed his hand, she felt an electric current rush through her veins, ending in a tiny explosion in her heart, making it skip a beat. There was much more to him than met the eye; she could feel it in her bones.

* * *

The ride home was quieter than the conversation on the beach. Still, it was peaceful to be with him, riding along in relative silence together, inching closer to the city.

Audrey was at a sleepover with her friend, Maya, and kid-free time was a rarity. So when Hassan pulled up to her apartment, Caroline threw her last bit of caution to the wind.

"Would you care to join me?" she asked, gesturing to her apartment building.

Without a word, he leaned in and wrapped his hand delicately around the back of her neck, pulling her in for a kiss. The explosion in her heart earlier seemed like a 4th of July sparkler compared to the inferno burning in her gut now as he kissed her.

"I would love to come inside," he whispered. "But you've had far too much to drink, and I can't have that on my conscience, should anything… untoward happen."

"What a gentleman you are, Mr. Soliman," she said, digging around in her purse for her keys while her face burned hot with embarrassment.

He got out of the car and came to her side to help her out of

CHAPTER 5

the car. Then he took her hand, kissing it gingerly. "Allow me to ensure that you make it inside safely Ms… what was your last name again?" he asked, letting her lead him up to the door.

"Rush."

"Well then, Ms. Rush, I hope you sleep well. Egg yolks and a shot of whiskey in the morning and you should be tip-top, okay?" he said, tucking her wind-swept hair behind her ear. "Meet me at that coffee shop later? Say around one o'clock?"

Caroline wasn't sure where this was going, or where *he hoped* it was going, but she liked the idea of spending more time with him. "If I survive the night, yes. That would be nice," she said, laughing, then turned the key and opened her squeaky door.

"Sleep well, Lina," he said, leaving her with a final, brief kiss.

Chapter 6

Caroline awoke to a throbbing headache. She reached for her phone and saw there were two missed calls from Mark, along with a text asking if she was having dinner with him. Nikki had also texted to say she'd drop Audrey off later that evening.

Through the hangover and brain fog, Caroline remembered Hassan and the evening they'd shared. She hadn't gotten his number, so there was no way to confirm their coffee date for later.

"Welp, I guess we'll see if he's such a stand-up guy after all," she said to her cat, Jericho, as she began making the egg yolk and whiskey concoction Hassan had recommended. She threw it back, and though it was awful, she *did*, indeed, begin to feel much better.

Caroline spent the rest of the morning cleaning her apartment and thinking about how she would end things with Mark. It wasn't something she could get out of by sending him a quick, *'Hey, sorry but we're not compatible'* letter in the mail. No, she had to bite the bullet and face it directly—and soon.

CHAPTER 6

Plus, she knew Audrey would have questions eventually when Mark stopped coming around. The thought of that conversation was even more unnerving than the one she needed to have with Mark.

And then there was Hassan. What sort of man turns down an invitation for a good time—well, maybe an *okay* time, considering how drunk she was, but still? Paul would have stayed the night with her, at least, to make sure she didn't suffocate in her own vomit in the night, and maybe he'd cop a feel if she seemed up to it.

By the time noon rolled around, she had convinced herself that Hassan was a figment of her imagination—a fairy tale knight who respects a woman's boundaries before she even attempts to establish them.

* * *

When Caroline walked in the door of the cafe, the new girl, Sarah, perked up and headed to the cash register, wiping her hands on her apron.

"Well, good morning, friend!" she beamed. "What can I get for you today?"

"Hey. Morning, Sarah," Caroline said, pushing her sunglasses up onto her head. "Can I get a tall dark roast?"

"Absolutely! Oh, and your check is in the back, by the way," she replied, getting started on Caroline's coffee.

Caroline glanced at her watch. It was 12:45 p.m. As she stood making conversation with her boss in the back room, all she could think of was whether Hassan would actually show up.

Her thoughts were interrupted by Antony, tapping her on the shoulder. "There's a gentleman at the register asking for you," he whispered. "Looks like he had a rough night, but he is *fine*, girl. Mmm!"

That he is, she thought to herself, imagining Hassan's picture-perfect smile. But as she turned the corner, she saw Mark standing at the register. His eyes were puffy and he wore a beanie to cover his messy auburn locks.

"Babe, I've been trying to reach you all morning. Is everything okay?" he asked, heading in for a kiss, but Caroline turned her cheek.

May as well get this over with, she thought.

"Hey, Mark. Let's sit down, okay?" she said, gesturing to a table at the far end of the cafe. She chose the seat facing the entrance, hoping she'd see Hassan come in before he saw her.

"What's up, babe?" Mark asked.

"Listen, I... think it's time we move on—" she began.

"Are you... *breaking up with me?*" Mark asked, tearing up before she got all the words out.

"I just think it's for the best, for everyone."

"But I *love* you, Caroline! And you know Audrey is my girl. We're buds!"

Caroline took a deep breath and steadied herself. She didn't want to tell him she had learned his little secret, so she tried to be as vague as possible. "Mark, it's not about love. I know you care for both of us, and yes Audrey likes you a lot. But... I think we've come to the end of this thing."

He seemed confused. "Did I... do something? Is it because I wanted you to come to my family Christmas? Caroline, we've been dating for *a year*."

"No, of course not. I love your family. It's... Okay, I don't

CHAPTER 6

know how else to say this, but I met someone else," she blurted out, lying through her teeth—sort of. *Well, that's one way to make sure he leaves you alone,* she thought. *Be the bad guy.*

Mark stood abruptly and pulled his jacket back on. "I see," he said, curtly. As he stood there, putting his phone in his pocket and making sure he had his wallet and keys, Caroline saw Hassan stroll through the front entrance. It was 1 p.m., on the dot.

And he's punctual?! she thought. *There is no way this man is real.*

"Can I kiss you, one last time?" Mark asked, softer now.

"I don't think that's a good idea," Caroline replied, half-hugging him and walking him to the side exit. "I'll drop off your stuff tomorrow, okay?"

He could tell she was rushing him out. "Caroline—" he began.

"I need to get home. Audrey is waiting," she lied, wishing he would just go already.

Now he was full-on crying as everyone, including Hassan, watched.

"Mark, *please*," Caroline said, taking him by the hand and leading him to his strawberry-red convertible outside.

"But I… I thought we were gonna *get married*, Caroline!" he cried, opening his glove compartment and taking out a small blue velvet box. He opened it, revealing a delicate, princess-cut solitaire on a gold band. It was beautiful, but he knew she *hated* gold, or at least she'd told him as much several times. It didn't matter now.

"Mark—" she began.

"It belonged to my great-grandmother. She brought it over from Poland! Poland, Caroline! It's vintage!"

"It's beautiful, really it is. And I'm flattered, but Mark... listen, we want different things. We have very different interests, okay?"

"Just because I don't like books?!" Mark sighed, snapping the ring box shut and stuffing it back in his glove compartment. "I'll read, Caroline! Just, give me a book and I'll read it, okay?" He was crying again.

Caroline knew there was something fundamentally *wrong* about how she felt inside, witnessing this scene. She didn't love Mark, that much she knew. But she had spent almost a year with him—nearly a full year of fun and laughter and tears, of being in his arms and having him in her bed, of making memories with him and her daughter. She knew she should have felt *something*, some ounce of empathy, but she couldn't even muster that.

Caroline turned and saw that Hassan was sitting at a table, patiently sipping his drink and trying to act like he—along with every other person in the building—wasn't watching with bated breath as the scene unfolded in the parking lot.

"I was gonna take you to Maui this winter and propose! Maui! Now what am I gonna do with those tickets, huh?!" Mark whined.

"I guess you could take Ali," Caroline said before she could stop herself.

Mark froze, mid-sentence, eyes wide open and confused. He was babbling something incoherent. Caroline worried he was having a stroke.

"I'm sorry. I didn't mean to... it just slipped out. I'm sorry. That wasn't—" Caroline said.

Without a word, Mark closed his passenger side door and walked around to the driver's side, climbed inside, and put the car in reverse. He pulled out of the parking lot and onto Glenoaks Boulevard, speeding away. And that was the last time Caroline would ever see him. Just like that, a year of her life was over, and a new chapter was about to begin.

Hassan approached her from behind. "You okay?" he asked gently.

"As okay as can be expected," she said, smoothing her hair behind her ears and willing her beat-red face to chill out already. "I bet that was awkward for you," she said, "I mean, watching that unfold."

"Me? Ha!" he said, chuckling. "That was the most exciting thing I've seen all month," he said, patting her on the shoulder. "But I imagine it wasn't so fun to experience."

She nodded, grimacing. "It was gonna happen eventually. Truthfully, he did me a favor by showing up. Got it done and over with. Though, I wish he hadn't cried so much."

"I'm sure he'll be okay. Are *you* okay?"

"I'll be fine. It wasn't too bad for me, as far as breakups go."

"Yeah, I guess it happens to even the best of us, though typically *not* because we found out our long-term partner is same-sex oriented." At that, they both laughed too loud for comfort in public. "You ready to get outta here?"

Caroline agreed, sliding her sunglasses down onto her nose.

"Your carriage, mi'lady, " Hassan said, offering her his arm and leading her to his BMW.

"*This* is what you drive?" she asked, side-eyeing him. "Why am I not surprised."

"Hey, don't hate on my sweet ride just because you drive a mom SUV."

She laughed inwardly at the "mom" comment. Once inside, she clicked her belt and got comfortable, letting down her messy bun and readjusting her sunglasses.

"Mind if we listen to some Arabic music?" he asked, shuffling through his playlist.

"Sure, but keep the volume do—" she started to say, but he was already blasting it, so she reached over and turned it down a few decibels. "Hangover, remember?" she said, pointing at her head.

He laughed and kissed her hand before they drove away.

7

Chapter 7

They spent the day driving north along Highway 1, exchanging stories. Their connection was as easy as it had been the night before. Hassan talked more about his travels, and she told him more about her life—though still avoiding the topic of Audrey.

Somewhere near Santa Barbara, Caroline was regaling him with a story about her Spring Break shenanigans in Miami one year when he looked over at her with those midnight eyes.

Her legs turned to jello. "What?" she asked. "Why are you looking at me like that?"

"The way the sun hits your face right now... It's *breathtaking*," he said, kissing his fingers in a chef's kiss.

Oh, he's good, she thought. "Hey, pull off here. I want to show you something."

He eyed her suspiciously but pulled off of the highway onto a smaller road.

"Keep driving," she directed him, as the asphalt gave way to gravel roads, and then to dirt roads. A few miles away from the coast, she asked him to pull off onto the shoulder.

The sun had just begun to set behind the ocean, filling the sky with deep purples and incandescent oranges. They were parked on the side of a nondescript dirt road—a place of no real appeal to most people, but it was *her spot*. She'd found it a year after Paul died when she had been driving mindlessly after yet another rejection of a screenplay she'd written. It quickly became her favorite thinking spot, her sanctuary.

"I had no idea there were places like this so close to the city!" Hassan exclaimed, taking in a deep breath.

"You like it? This is nothing compared to Indiana, my good man. Real, dirty Indiana. There are spots there that could make you cry, they're so pretty."

"Interesting. So you really *are* a country girl, then. I have a sweet spot for country girls..." he replied, smiling flirtatiously.

This time, Caroline didn't wait for him to make a move. She grabbed him by the collar and pulled him in for a long, sensual kiss. "Got a little problem there?" she whispered, noticing the growing bulge in his jeans.

"Ha!" he laughed, lifting his body awkwardly from his seat to adjust himself.

"Right about now I bet you're wishing we drove my lame Mom SUV," she laughed.

"I'd lose that bet," he replied, lifting her skirt and stroking her inner thigh. "I *could* take you back to my place."

"Now that's bold of you. How do you know I *want* to go back to your place? This *is* only our first official date, after all."

"Tell me I'm wrong," he whispered, his breath hot on her neck.

Caroline shuddered in response.

"But then, I guess there's something about being in a car, you know? Worrying you could be caught kinda adds to the

CHAPTER 7

experience," he continued.

"Oh, you're *dangerous*," Caroline laughed, pulling him into the backseat with her.

* * *

A week later, Hassan took her out dancing at a club in Hollywood. Surrounded by women half her age wearing half as much clothing as she was, Hassan made her feel like the most desirable woman that had ever lived. The bouncing music, the strobing lights, the way he smelled—all of it worked like magic. Caroline Rush felt *alive* for the first time. When he invited her back to his place that time, she didn't have to think twice.

Making love to Hassan felt much like talking with him did—like *coming home.* His body fit perfectly against hers as if they'd been lovers for lifetimes. He whispered strange, foreign things in her ear and she didn't need to understand the words to know what he was saying.

Afterward, the two of them got dressed and stepped outside on his balcony while Caroline smoked a cigarette. "Want one?" she offered.

"Naw, I can't stand the things," Hassan replied. "But thank you."

Now's as good a time as any, she thought to herself. "Hey listen. I need to tell you something," she began. "And I need you not to freak out, okay?"

Hassan stiffened up a bit. "Don't tell me you're married. Was Mark just a side-piece?" he said, stifling a laugh.

"*Real funny,*" she replied. "But no. I'm not married. I came close once, but he died."

His face was serious now. "Oh, Lina. I'm sorry for your loss. *Inna lillahi wa inna ilayhi rajioon*, we say when someone dies. It means *'We came from God, and we return to God.'*"

"Thank you," she replied. "But there's more. We had a daughter—*have* a daughter. Audrey. She's ten years old now. She's staying with my friend, Nikki, this weekend. But yeah... I have a daughter."

Hassan dropped his hand from hers and took a few steps away.

"Look, I know this is a big deal," she said. "I would understand if you preferred to end... whatever this could become." She was prepared to hear the same tired, lazy excuses she heard from the other dozens of cowards she'd attempted to date since Paul died.

"Lina, of course not. This doesn't end anything," he said, gazing into her eyes. "I'm actually relieved."

"Relieved?" she asked, confused.

"I guess now it's my turn to share my secret," he said, running a hand through his hair.

"You're not gay, are you? Because hey, do what makes you happy. But I've had my fair share of *that* story lately!" she laughed.

He laughed, too. "Nope. Not at all. But, I think I may be sterile. I've not officially had it checked out, but my ex and I tried for children for a few years and had no luck."

Caroline took his hand in hers. "That's hardly a reason to think you're sterile, Hassan."

"She got pregnant a few months later, with her new boyfriend."

"Oh."

"Yeah," he sighed. "I've always wanted to be a father. So."

CHAPTER 7

"I can only imagine how devastating that was for you."

Hassan took a deep breath. "So, knowing that you have your daughter... if whatever this is becomes something more, I'd so much love to get to know her, if you'd allow it."

"I'm glad you feel that way," she replied, beaming. This guy *really* was too good to be true. "So glad."

* * *

Caroline drove home from his house the next morning, smiling like an idiot. When she pulled into her driveway, Nikki was already there.

"You seem happy," Nikki said, eyeing Caroline suspiciously.

"Yeah... so much to tell you!" Caroline replied before grabbing Audrey in a bear hug.

"*Mommm,* you're gonna ruin my hair!" Audrey whined, re-adjusting her hair and grabbing her book bag from the back seat.

After Audrey and Maya headed inside, Caroline sat with Nikki on the back deck of her apartment while she caught Nikki up-to-speed on recent happenings.

"So you've upgraded from a spoiled rich white dude to a spoiled rich Arab one," Nikki said.

"Well, when you put it that way..." Caroline replied, rolling her eyes.

"Hey, no shame! Whatever gets your engine going. But how are you gonna break the news to Audrey? About Mark, I mean."

Caroline had nearly forgotten about that impending conversation—nearly forgotten all about Mark, in truth.

"I guess I'm just gonna be as honest as I can. And anyway, once she meets Hassan, she'll forget all about Mark. He's so much more interesting. She'll love him."

Nikki took a long sip of water and sat her glass down on the deck.

"What? What are you thinking?" Caroline asked. She could always tell when Nikki was holding back.

"I just worry about you. It feels like maybe you're rushing this thing."

"Yeah?"

"Listen, in all the time I've known you, you've never taken more than 2.5 seconds between men to like... *breathe*. And you usually give in and bring Audrey into things far too early."

Caroline sighed and sat with her face in her hands. She knew Nikki was right, but that didn't make it easier to hear. "Okay. I see your point. Especially about Audrey. But it's not like we're *engaged*. I've only known him for a week. It was a spectacular fuck, Nikki, that's all. Don't I *deserve* a spectacular fuck from time to time?"

"You deserve much more than that, honey. And I don't know if you'll ever find it if you keep rushing things like this."

"What can I say? Rush is my last name, after all. It's in my blood."

"Mmm-hm," Nikki said, snickering. "Keep telling yourself that." With that, she pulled Caroline in for a hug, and called Maya out to head home.

After Nikki and Maya left, Caroline sat alone on the deck, smoking a quick cigarette. When she was finished, she went inside and ordered Indian take-out for lunch.

She and Audrey cuddled up on the couch, eating and

CHAPTER 7

laughing together as they watched an old favorite of Audrey's.

"So you finally figured out that Mark bats for the other team?" Audrey said between shoveling naan and spoonfuls of chicken tikka masala and rice in her mouth.

"Audrey!" Caroline cried. "How—"

"Mom, your voice carries. And I'm nosy, okay?"

"And what do you mean *finally figured out*? Is there something you know that I don't?"

"Many things," Audrey laughed. "You're just blind."

"So you're not... sad?"

"Course I'm sad. He was a cool guy. But it's not like I have to stop hanging out with him just because you broke up with him."

"That's *exactly* what it means."

Audrey stood to refill her cup of Root Beer. "Okay, Mom. Whatever you say. But you can't stop him from coming to my soccer games. The park is public property."

"Fair."

"Now shut up so we can finish this movie," she said, patting Caroline's leg.

Well, that was easier than I imagined, Caroline thought.

Chapter 8

Just as Nikki had prophesied, Caroline introduced Audrey to Hassan far too quickly. But at least this time, it wasn't her fault.

It happened on a regular Thursday evening, three months after they'd met. Audrey was fast asleep while Caroline and Hassan were snuggled up in bed, watching the latest "Lord of the Rings" movie and eating greasy pizza.

Suddenly, Audrey burst into the room, rubbing her eyes and shielding them against the brightness of the TV. "Mom, there is a *huge* spider in the bathr—" she started. Then she saw him, sitting stiff as a board next to Caroline.

"Honey, let's go kill your spider," Caroline said, rushing Audrey out of the room and killing the spider.

"So, *that* just happened..." Hassan remarked when Caroline climbed back into bed a few minutes later.

"Yeah... I'll have to deal with that situation in the morning," she said. "Sorry about that. I didn't think she would bust in like that without even knocking."

Hassan smiled sweetly. "Don't apologize for your daughter

CHAPTER 8

needing you."

"I don't know what to tell her," Caroline said, worried.

"Just tell her the truth: we're dating," Hassan suggested.

"Oh, is *that* what's happening here, sir?" she said, smiling.

"Indeed. For now," he replied, pulling her in closer.

* * *

The next morning at breakfast, with Hassan long gone, Caroline sat with Audrey at the table, trying to feel things out. "So, did you sleep well?" she asked.

Audrey was not amused. "Who was in your bed last night?" she asked, casually taking a sip of her tea and buttering a piece of toast.

For the thousandth time since the doctors handed Audrey to her ten years before, Caroline was astonished by her daughter.

"Okay then, let's dive right in, shall we?" she replied. "His name is Hassan."

"Go on."

"He's from Kansas City and he travels a lot for work."

"Uh-huh."

"And we've been dating for several months now. He treats me well, and he's respectful and lots of fun. He's super curious about you, too."

"Like Mark was?" she asked. "Not that *that* mattered much in the end."

"Fair point. Low blow, but... yeah."

Audrey took a deep breath and another sip of tea. "I don't mind, Mom," she said, relaxing now. "Just, please don't let him move in."

"We've just started dating, Audrey. And come on, Mark

never moved in and we were together for a whole year!"

"Promise, Mom."

Caroline sighed. "Scouts' honor," she said, holding up her best Girl Scout pledge.

"Also, I'd like an official 'meet the daughter' date at a nice dinner place, if you'll be so kind as to pass that request along to your gentleman caller," Audrey said, emptying the remaining tea in her mug into the sink. Without waiting for Caroline's answer, she popped into the bathroom to get ready for school.

* * *

Two weeks later, Hassan took the two of them out to dinner at a snazzy Italian place in Santa Monica. Against all odds, Audrey liked him, right away. Within a few months, they were like two peas in a pod. They both loved soccer, which meant Caroline's house was frequently filled with Audrey's classmates and Hassan's friends, screaming and cheering and throwing popcorn everywhere. Caroline was *delighted.*

But their favorite thing to do together was play pranks on Caroline. Once, she walked into the living room, drying her hair mindlessly with a towel, when the two of them jumped out from behind the couch and covered her, head to toe, in Silly String.

Another time, when Mimi was in town, Caroline hurried to Audrey's soccer match only to discover it had been canceled, and Mimi, Hassan, and Audrey had snuck away to the arcade to have fun without her.

Mimi liked him, Audrey adored him, and Caroline was head over heels in love with him. And yet, Hassan continued to rent

CHAPTER 8

his apartment in the hills, and Audrey continued to enjoy her space in the house with Caroline.

Then one day, just shy of a year into their relationship, while Caroline was away for the weekend at a writer's conference, Audrey and Hassan conspired to move Hassan's things into the house. Everything, from the living room furniture to his clothes in her closet and his toiletries in her bathroom, had been placed just so—as if it had been there all along. Caroline set her bags down and looked around, baffled but smiling.

She found them outside on the back deck, cooking hot dogs and cheeseburgers on the grill. "So… it looks like someone pulled a reverse thievery at our house and left a bunch of furniture and clothes instead of taking any of our stuff?" she asked.

"Odd, huh? It was like that when I woke up this morning," Audrey mumbled casually, not looking up from her video game.

Caroline eyed Hassan, who shrugged and made a *'Hey, it wasn't my idea'* grin.

And that was that.

II

Part Two

9

Chapter 9

Two Years Later

When Caroline stepped off the plane onto the stairs on the tarmac in Cairo, she was hit with a blast of hot, dry air. It smelled the way she imagined Mars would smell: like she'd stuck her head into a freshly baked clay pot.

Two years after she bumped into Hassan outside Mark's bedroom door, the three of them had gone on a whirlwind vacation, gallivanting from Paris to Budapest then Rome, and rounded it all out in Cairo. Caroline and Audrey were finally going to meet Hassan's family. He'd booked them all tickets on a lazy cruise down the Nile, from Cairo to Luxor.

"Mom, wait for me!" Audrey said, pulling her suitcase behind her.

Caroline slowed her pace a bit and held out her hand for her daughter, then stood on her tip-toes to see where Hassan had gone. She found him talking to someone who looked to be his younger brother.

"Lina, Audrey, *ta'ali*," Hassan said, rushing them. "Majed has the car waiting for us out front. They'll give him a huge fine if we don't hurry."

They were surrounded by reunited lovers and family members, as well as businessmen searching for their drivers. People from all different countries spoke in a hundred different languages at once, wearing colorful clothes with patterns that dazzled the eye—a cacophony of cultures.

Audrey took it all in, looking this way and that in awe and curiosity like she had every day since their round-the-world trip began three months before in Paris. Caroline had worried about how Audrey would handle so much travel at her age, but she'd been managing it all like a champ.

Though Hassan's father had loved Caroline and Audrey when Hassan took them to meet him in Kansas City the summer before, they hadn't met the rest of his family yet. Majed was busy with his legal practice in Dallas, while his twin sister, Marwa, and their elder sister, Hafsa, had gone to Cairo with their mother to visit family, as they did every summer.

A few weeks after that trip to Kansas City, Caroline had overheard Hassan and his father talking on the phone about how his mother was desperately trying to find him a wife in Egypt before he fell in love with "that American woman with her daughter." By then, though, it was too late—far, far too late.

Needless to say, Caroline wasn't exactly thrilled to be meeting the rest of the family, but it had to happen sooner or later, so she tried to hope for the best and prepare herself

CHAPTER 9

for the worst.

As they caught up with Hassan and Majed ahead, Hassan introduced them and then helped her and Audrey into the waiting SUV. After he threw their suitcases into the back hatch, he jumped into the front seat next to Majed.

The first thing Caroline noticed was the lack of seat belts. The next thing was the almost total disregard anyone showed for stoplights. Like the other drivers on the clogged road, Majed didn't seem concerned about honoring the posted speed limit, either. Caroline was a nervous wreck, but Audrey seemed positively *thrilled*.

Hassan and Majed were chatting animatedly in Arabic in the front seat. Caroline had learned a few words by now, but this was rapid-fire banter, so she had no idea what was being discussed.

Finally, Majed turned his attention to them. "How has your trip been, *habibti*?" he asked Audrey.

"Pretty great!" she said, smiling from ear to ear. "Much better use of my summer than laying around our house all day, that's for sure."

"Of course! You're so brave, *mashaAllah*. That's a big trip for so small a girl."

"I'm not *that* small," Audrey smiled, pushing her hair behind her ear in the way she did. "I'm nearly thirteen." Everyone laughed.

"And you, Lina? What do you think of Egypt so far?" Majed asked, smiling.

"Well, I just got off the plane," she said, laughing awkwardly. "But it's nothing like I imagined. I guess I thought there would be older buildings, more temples."

"Oh, no. That's only Giza, where the pyramids are, and

Luxor, which is pretty far south. That's where the Temple of Karnak is and the Valley of the Kings."

"When are we going there?" Audrey asked Hassan. She was bouncing with excitement.

He smiled and reached around to pat her leg. "Next week, *habibti*."

* * *

What had frightened Caroline most—the prospect of meeting Hassan's mother—turned out to be the easiest part. Without so much as a "hello," she threw her arms around Caroline and Audrey and kissed them on both cheeks, several times, repeating what sounded like sweet words in Arabic.

It was Hassan's eldest sister, Hafsa—who was ten years his senior—that turned out to be the least welcoming of the Soliman clan. After their initial introduction, she never initiated conversation and seemed annoyed by their presence. Much more religious than the rest of the family—who always offered wine and champagne with dinner—Hafsa scoffed and mumbled prayers under her breath as the rest of the family indulged happily.

But where Hafsa was cold and unavailable, Hassan's younger sister, Marwa, was the life of the party. At 21 years old, she was finishing up her final year of college at the University of Kansas. She and Audrey were instant friends. During their week-long stay in the Soliman house in Cairo before their Nile cruise, they stayed awake for hours into the night laughing like hyenas, doing one another's makeup, and gossiping like old friends.

CHAPTER 9

* * *

Eight days into the ten-day cruise along the Nile from Cairo to Luxor, Caroline stood on the deck of the cruise liner, watching the sun go down.

Hassan approached her from behind and kissed her on the neck. "It's incredible, isn't it?" he remarked as he slid his arms around her waist and pushed himself against her bottom. "The scenery isn't bad, either."

Caroline laughed. "You are shameless Mr. Soliman," she replied, pushing her body against his and enjoying the warmth. Since she and Audrey shared a cabin while he shared one with Majed, there had been no intimacy or much affection at all, as it was frowned upon in his culture, Hassan said.

"I'm not sure I can wait until we get back to L.A. I may have to drag you into my cabin when Majed isn't around and have my way with you," he whispered.

"Tsk tsk tsk..." she clucked. "What would your mama think if she knew you spoke like this—and to an unmarried woman, no less!"

"It's funny you bring that up," he replied, more serious now.

As she turned toward him, he dropped to one knee and her stomach dropped with him.

"Oh God, Hassan," she whispered through tears. Several people stopped to watch the scene unfolding.

"Habibti, Lina. Love of my life. Please, do me the honor—" he started.

"Yes, I'll marry you! Of course!" she cried, pulling him to his feet and kissing him.

The small crowd on deck had increased to more than a dozen

people now, his family and Audrey among them.

Audrey marched right up to Hassan and threw her arms around his neck. "Finally!" she said. "I thought you'd never do it! You were *supposed* to propose back in Paris!"

Hassan laughed and pulled Audrey in for a hug, before handing her a small box with a locket inside. It contained a picture of the three of them in front of the Parthenon, taken a few short weeks ago.

"You knew this whole time? And didn't tell me?!" Caroline asked Audrey.

She giggled and threw her arms around her mother's neck. "Comrades don't share comrades' secrets, Mother," she replied seriously. "Plus, I wanted to see the look on your face. You had no idea!"

After the congratulations, the crowd dispersed and the three of them stood together, looking out across the Egyptian countryside as the Nile flowed beneath them.

* * *

The following night, Caroline awoke from a bad dream, unable to fall back asleep. So she climbed out of bed, wrapped herself in a warm shawl, and stepped out onto the deck of the ship, thinking maybe a stroll would tire her out.

The midnight air was warm and moist against her skin. Bullfrogs were croaking along the banks of the Nile and the sound of the boat churning along in the water was rhythmic and soothing. If she closed her eyes, she could imagine herself in a movie, surveying the darkness beyond as she plunged into her new future, unaware of what was coming around the bend.

CHAPTER 9

Could be a good screenplay idea, she thought, absentmindedly.

As she walked past Majed and Hassan's cabin, she overheard them talking, and they weren't alone. Against her better judgment, she lingered outside the cabin, listening. Most of the conversation was in Arabic, but she picked out a few words she knew. Whatever they were saying, it was about her and Audrey and the fact they were American.

"Think of Audrey," Marwa chimed in, switching to English. "If it doesn't work between you two, Audrey will be *devastated*. *Haraam*, she doesn't deserve that."

Hassan was silent for a moment. "Listen," he said. "I know she isn't what you wanted for me, Mama. But—"

His mother interrupted him, her voice sounding harsh and angry—or at least that's what Caroline thought, as they had switched back to Arabic.

Just then, Hassan raised his voice, interrupting his mother. Caroline wasn't sure if she *wanted* to know what he was saying. He'd only raised his voice at her once in all the time she'd known him, and he immediately apologized. Whatever his mother had said, it had to have been something *big* to make him react like that.

Caroline worried they would open the door and find her eavesdropping, so she turned back to her cabin. She didn't need that midnight stroll on deck, after all. Once in her cabin, Caroline lay awake until dawn, nervously fidgeting with the ring on her finger and crying.

Growing up without a mother, she'd always dreamed of being enveloped in the warm arms of a mother-in-law who would welcome her into the family. Paul's mother had been a cold alcoholic who cursed at her whenever Caroline tried to help her with anything. She'd hoped the next time around she'd have better luck, but it didn't look like it was in the cards for her.

* * *

The cruise ship finally arrived in Luxor the next morning. Audrey and Caroline marveled at the ancient ruins of the Temple of Karnak and the sights and sounds of the bustling, ancient metropolis. They especially enjoyed the night tour and light show at the Luxor Temple.

After a few days of rest in their five-star resort, their group traveled northwest from the Nile to visit The Valley of the Kings. Caroline took dozens of pictures of Audrey smiling in front of statues of Egyptian gods and the sarcophagi of pharaohs spread throughout the valley.

Audrey's favorite was the Temple of Hatshepsut. She rattled off fun facts she had learned on the plane ride over, dazzling other visitors, like a mini-tour guide.

"Did you know," she said, climbing up the stairs to the temple with Caroline and Hassan and his family, "that Hatshepsut wasn't *just* the first and most successful female Pharaoh of Kemet, but she was a cross-dresser?" When the group gasped, she went on. "That's right! She wore a fake beard and a traditional *shendyt* and crown for her official Pharaohnic depictions, to give an air of authority. And she ruled for twenty years!"

* * *

CHAPTER 9

Much as she enjoyed watching Audrey make such memories, the rest of the trip was bittersweet for Caroline. She couldn't stop thinking about the conversation she'd overheard on the cruise. *What had they said? Why was he so upset?*

She waited for Hassan to be ready to open up to her, or even to call the whole thing off. But that moment never came. To everyone but Caroline, it was as if the midnight conversation never happened.

The night before they were set to fly back to L.A., as Hassan was brushing his teeth in the bathroom while Caroline sat on the edge of the bed, rubbing lotion on her legs, she opened the subject.

"Just tell me why they seem so opposed to the wedding," Caroline said.

"They aren't *opposed*. They just wish I would have married an Egyptian girl. Or at least another Arab," Hassan said, spitting toothpaste into the sink and rinsing his mouth out with water. "And are you just gonna bulldoze over my feelings about you listening in? We were *speaking Arabic*, behind closed doors, in the middle of the night. That's three clear signs we were having a *private* conversation."

"I... didn't realize you thought it was okay for us to keep secrets from one another, because I certainly didn't."

Hassan sighed dramatically. "Lina, it's not a *secret*. Jesus. Asking for privacy isn't some absurd, excessive request. I was talking to *my family*."

"Yes, your family who doesn't want you to marry me. Because they hate me."

"Baby, they don't *hate you*. They actually like you and they *adore* Audrey, okay? They just have some old-fashioned ideas about interfaith marriages and stuff like that."

"So they're mad that I'm not Muslim? That doesn't even make any sense! Except for Hafsa, no one in your family even *prays their daily prayers*, Hassan."

Hassan turned the lights off in the bathroom and sat in a chair next to the bed. "You don't understand. Religion isn't a *personal* thing here, Lina. It's a family thing, a *cultural* thing. Even if you only pray and fast during Ramadan, you're still Muslim. Unless you're Coptic, in which case... well, they aren't all that different from us, not really."

"What do you mean?"

"I mean... boys will be boys. We're gonna sow our wild oats, as far and as wide as we can. And the more scandalous the girl, the better. It's the thrill of knowing you're doing something doubly bad, I guess. I dunno."

"That's childish," Caroline said.

"Yes! That's the point! It's childish. That's why when it comes time to *marry*, you settle down with a good girl your family approves of."

"And they won't approve of me unless I convert to Islam?"

Hassan laughed out loud. "Mama would be *thrilled*, but no one else would take you seriously. We grew up in *America*, baby. Majed and the girls... they'd know you only did it to placate my mother. We all know at least one white girl who thinks marrying a Muslim man and wearing a head scarf to the mosque a few times a year entitles her to claim she's an *oppressed minority*," he said, rolling his eyes. "The only thing worse in in their eyes than you being a white girl is you converting for me."

"So, I'm damned if I do, damned if I don't?" Caroline asked, exasperated.

"Not to me you're not. Though you are *devilishly sexy*, I'll

CHAPTER 9

give you that much," Hassan said, pulling her in for a kiss and turning off the bedside lamp.

And that was all they ever said about it.

Chapter 10

A few days after they arrived home from their trip, Caroline awoke in the middle of the night with horrible stomach pain.

"Maybe you caught something? Tell me you only drank the bottled water, baby," Hassan asked when he awoke and found her there, sleeping on the bathroom floor in her robe.

But Caroline knew it wasn't the water. Her period had been due three days before, but she'd chalked it up to jet lag and exhaustion. She took a test alone that night after Hassan had fallen asleep. Doctors be damned, his seed wasn't dead, after all.

The next morning, after Audrey went to her first day of the new term, Caroline sat with Hassan at the dining table and told him the news.

"I can't believe it! I... are you sure?" he asked, nervous and giddy all at once. He picked her up off the ground and danced her around the house.

The next test confirmed the first results, as did the blood test her doctor performed a week later.

CHAPTER 10

* * *

For the next several months, Caroline basked in the light of his pride and adoration, simultaneously thrilled and nervous.

Pregnancy is never easy, but this one was so much harder than her pregnancy with Audrey. She couldn't keep anything but saltines down, and the debilitating headaches and nausea kept her in bed most days. But she wrote it all off as normal, considering how much older she was now than when she had Audrey.

Right on schedule, the morning sickness stopped after the first trimester and she began to feel better. But when she went for her 16-week sonogram, there was another explanation for the sudden stop in symptoms: her fetus had no heartbeat.

Hassan cried as he drove them home. For days, Caroline stayed alone in their room while her body expelled the pregnancy. She told Audrey an innocent fib about having had a minor procedure done to explain what was happening.

* * *

Six months after they lost the baby, the wedding went off without a hitch, and no one was the wiser. It was a small, simple affair in a local mosque, followed by a much grander reception at her favorite Japanese garden. Hassan's family flew in from Kansas City, and Caroline's father and Mimi made it, too.

It was a weekend full of love and hope, simple as it was, but the light that had been draining from Hassan's eyes since the day she lost the baby was nearly extinguished as they rode away to their honeymoon on Catalina Island.

In his defense, Hassan *tried* to give Caroline a good time. They spent their days visiting the cute shops in the touristy town of Avalon, and spent their nights relaxing in the hot tub outside their suite.

It was pleasant after such a hard year. But there was a marked distance between the two of them, a thick veil that permitted neither warmth nor affection.

* * *

Months later, the light still hadn't returned to Hassan's eyes. When they did make love, which wasn't nearly as frequently as Caroline preferred, it was a slow, methodical affair that left them both disappointed.

"I don't know what to do," Caroline confided in her friend, Sharice, one evening on a video call, the two of them sipping their separate wines, two thousand miles apart. They'd grown up together, but Sharice had escaped their small Indiana town before Caroline had, starting a boutique bakery in Chicago the same year Audrey was born.

"Girl, that man is his *own person*. He has his own grief to work through," she replied, adding, "Plus, men are just weird about shit like this."

"But there must be something I could do to bridge the gap," Caroline responded. She'd tried all her old tried-and-true methods to coax him out of his isolation, but nothing seemed to cool the icy wall between them.

"He needs some time away from you, away from Audrey,

CHAPTER 10

away from his stressful job. Send him away on a boys' trip or something."

Sharice always knew best.

Caroline suggested it a few days later, over dinner, and the effect was instant.

"What?" Hassan asked, confused. "You think I should go away?"

"Hey, I'm not throwing you out," she said, laughing. "It just seems like you could do with some time with the guys, some kid-free and wife-free time. It's been a while since you did that."

"Yeah, you're right. It *has* been a long while," he said, taking a sip of his water. "Lemme see what Jory and Malik are up to. Maybe Eric can even get away from his wife and the twins for a day or two."

"Ha! Unlikely," Caroline remarked. "You and I both know Denise is *not* the 'go away with the boys honey, I'll hold down the fort' kinda wife."

He smiled big and stood, crossing the room to her. He lifted her chin so she was looking into his eyes. The light within them began to flicker back to life.

"Thank God you are, Lina," he whispered, kissing her eyelids. "Thank you, *habibti*."

* * *

So Hassan went away with the boys—sans Eric who, of course, couldn't get away. They were gone for a week, at a resort in Puerto Rico. The reception was awful where he was, so other than a few texts, she didn't hear from him the whole week. Though she was glad for him to get a break, the loneliness she had been carrying since the miscarriage seemed to seep even deeper into her bones.

The night he arrived home, Caroline was ready for him. After dropping Audrey at a friend's house for the night, she got busy. First, she bought herself some new lingerie she knew he would like, then she spent all evening cleaning so the house would be immaculate for him. After she finished cleaning, she took a long shower, shaving and waxing everything just the way he liked it, then rinsed out the tub and started a bubble bath so he would find her there, waiting for him.

Right on time, she heard the front door open and close and the familiar sound of his keys clinking against the metal bowl on the small table next to the front door. He called for her throughout the house before finally wandering into their bathroom.

"What have we here?" he asked playfully when he saw her.

"A welcoming party," she smiled flirtatiously. She stood slowly and let the bubbles cascade down her body as she leaned forward and kissed him. He moaned in longing and reached for her breasts, but she moved his hands away. "No clothes for me, no clothes for you. Those are the rules."

"Oh, are they?" he asked, as he was undressing. "Says who?"

"The queen of this bathroom."

"More like the queen of my heart," he said, climbing into the tub and taking her in his arms. Without another word, he roughly bent her over the side of the bathtub and entered her. After only a few strokes, he emptied himself into her. And then they were done.

It certainly wasn't what she envisioned when she started the day, and it wasn't anything like the consummate pleasure she usually enjoyed with him. Hassan was always gentle, and he always made sure she was satisfied before he allowed himself to succumb. But at least his passion was a welcome return.

"I have a surprise for you," he said, grabbing his phone from the bedside table as he dried his thick hair with a towel. "I rented it for you, for next weekend. You can go alone, or invite Sharice, or take Nikki or Maria with you. Whatever. But leave Audrey here. There's a tournament on, and I promised her we'd watch it with her friends on the big screen downstairs."

The pictures of the exterior of the cabin were impressive: a small, quaint, A-frame, two hours north of Chicago on Lake Michigan, near Wind Point, Wisconsin. With two small bedrooms, it was perfect for her and Sharice, who took no convincing when Caroline called and invited her the next morning.

11

Chapter 11

"Are you sure this is the right place?" Sharice asked. With traffic and a storm that rolled in, their trip had taken much longer than they thought it would. Now, it was well after dark when they pulled into the driveway. "I'm not trying to get shot in the middle of nowhere, Wisconsin for the crime of being Black while knocking on the wrong door."

A small bronze plaque, emblazoned with the words "Lighthouse Reach" hung on the front door.

"No, this is definitely the place," Caroline replied, pulling her phone out to let Hassan and Audrey know they'd arrived safely.

After getting their bags from the back of the rental car, they walked up the steps to the front door, using their phone flashlights to navigate through the darkness. Once inside, Caroline flipped a switch on the wall in the entryway, but no lights turned on.

"Ugh, a power outage? Really?" Sharice whined. "Why me?!"

"I'll message the owner and let them know," Caroline said, setting her bags down next to the couch in the living room.

CHAPTER 11

A few minutes later, the owner replied, apologizing and telling her where to find matches and candles, flashlights, and an emergency generator should the outage last into the next day.

After admiring the quaint coziness of the place—or what they could make out of it in the darkness—they found their way to their rooms and turned in for the night.

The room Caroline chose sat on the far corner of the house, with an entire wall of windows facing east toward the lake below. She watched as some geese landed on the lake in the moving light of the lighthouse on the hill, south of the cabin. She fell asleep to the sound of crickets chirping outside her window and the waves lapping against the shore below.

* * *

Bright and early on Saturday morning, Caroline awoke to the sun pouring hot through the windows onto her face. She sat up in bed, stretching and admiring her room for the weekend. The soft linens and gentle textures of the room absorbed the morning light, creating a cocoon of warmth.

When she opened her bedroom door and walked into the central living area, her heart stopped. Now, in the light of day, the cabin was *magnificent*. The room itself was modern and minimalist with its clean lines and simple elegance. A vintage armchair, with its faded fabric and sturdy frame, was positioned just so in the light. Built-in bookshelves lined the walls, surrounding the stately stone fireplace in the center of the eastern wall. There were plants everywhere, from floor to ceiling. It felt like standing in a living library.

After Caroline got the fire going, she browsed the bookshelves, settling on a Jane Austen novel. She made herself comfortable in the old armchair and lost herself in 1800s England.

"That sun is rude as fuck," Sharice said as she wandered from her bedroom an hour later, rubbing her eyes. "Clearly, Mr. Sun didn't get the memo that I am *on vacation, thank you very much.*"

Caroline laughed and headed into the kitchen to make some coffee. Mugs in hand, the two of them walked out on the back deck, wrapped in flannel throw blankets Sharice grabbed from the back of the couch.

"I thought we'd take a hike this morning," Caroline said.

"No way. I am *not* trudging through that muddy, leafy mess. I love you, but no."

"*Come on*, it'll be great! We can get some good pictures! Isn't it about time you updated your Tinder profile?"

"Hey, I'll have you know that things are going just fine on that front. Jayden and I have been dating for a month now."

"Oooh, *a whole month!*" Caroline said sarcastically.

Sharice was not amused. "You know that's like six months for me."

"Shall we book the church then? Or... isn't Jayden Buddhist? How do they get married, anyway?"

Sharice scoffed. "No one said a damn word about marriage."

Caroline smiled and finished off her coffee. "Fine then. I guess I'll just have to go out into the wild unknown all by my lonesome. You think there's like... bears out here?" she asked, gesturing around vaguely.

"I dunno, but I pity the bear who finds *you* in these woods,"

Sharice said. "If you need me, I'll be snuggled up on *that* couch, reading a book and sipping wine all afternoon. But let's have dinner tonight?"

"Sounds like a plan, Stan."

Caroline went inside and dressed for the trek, thankful she'd had the mind to bring along her good-quality hiking boots. Picking up her phone, she saw she'd missed a call from Audrey.

"Everything good?" Caroline texted Audrey.

"Yep. We're gonna watch a football game later on TV, and he said I could invite my friends, too."

"That's good to hear. Have fun!"

"Hey Mom," Audrey texted.

"Yeah?"

"Why didn't you have any more kids?"

Caroline nearly dropped the phone. They'd never told Audrey about the miscarriage, and the timing was odd, to say the least.

When Caroline didn't respond right away, Audrey texted her again. "Did you see how awesome I was and decide I'm more than enough?"

Caroline laughed to herself, thinking it wasn't half-wrong. "Yep, that's it. What made you ask this?"

"I dunno. All my friends have siblings."

"Let's talk more about this when I get back."

Audrey texted back a quick "K" and a kissy-face emoji.

Caroline put her phone into the front pocket of her backpack, tossed in a few bags of trail mix and a bottle of water, laced up her boots, and set out down the stairs behind the house.

* * *

Caroline walked all along the coast that day, enjoying the scenery and the freedom to *just be*, with no agenda. The crunching leaves below, the ocean-blue sky above, the smell of earth in the air—nothing quite perked her up like a hike. It would have been fun to traipse with Sharice through the woods, but as she walked, she realized how badly she needed some solitude.

As the sun moved across the sky, she walked on, stopping now and then to nibble on her trail mix and take a few long gulps of water, maybe take a picture of a tree she particularly liked, along with countless shots of the coastline.

She couldn't help but think of Hassan and what he and Audrey were up to, and of the screenplay she'd left on her desk in her office at home, much as she'd wanted to bring it with her. That one had *promise,* she was sure of it.

As she sat on a large boulder trying to catch her breath, she couldn't stop thinking about what Audrey had said about wanting a sibling. The memory of losing her pregnancy washed over her. The pain began spilling out of her eyes and choking her.

A branch snapped behind her, so she turned toward the sound.

"Sorry to startle you," the man said, approaching slowly. "Are you hurt? I heard you crying while I was walking. Did you fall?"

Caroline wiped her eyes in embarrassment. "No, I'm... I'm fine. Sorry to disturb you."

He smiled and extended his hand. "Name's Rob. You new to the area?"

"No, not exactly. We're renting a cabin for the weekend." She dusted off her jeans and wiped the mascara from under

CHAPTER 11

her eyes.

"Oh, yeah. Mr. Harrison's place, right?"

"Yeah. Anyway, I'd better head back. Sharice will worry about me."

"I have to head that way myself," he replied. "Mind if I walk with you?"

He seemed polite and the sun was falling behind the horizon, so she agreed. He knew the way better than her, anyway, so he could be a good help.

As the two of them walked toward her cabin, he made polite conversation, asking if she'd been to the lighthouse yet and such. He asked what she and her "partner" thought about the area, so she explained that Sharice was *not* her partner. She didn't tell him she indeed *had* a partner. She'd left her rings in the glass dish on the counter in the bathroom, as she didn't want to risk losing them or muddying them on the hike.

Rob wasn't her type by any stretch, but there was something warm about him, something that felt inviting. And he had the most gorgeous green eyes. Not that she was looking, of course.

"Well, I hope you enjoy your time here," he said, interrupting her thoughts.

"Thanks for the company, and sorry again for my messy display. It's been a rough year."

He smiled. "Ah. Yes. One of those years? I've had a few myself. Good evening, Ms…"

"Oh, sorry. I'm Caroline," she said.

"Caroline. Lovely name! Have a good evening, *Caroline*."

The way he lingered on her name gave her an odd feeling in her gut—almost a pleasant one, but it made her feel guilty.

Chapter 12

While they ate at the steakhouse that evening, Sharice shared her couch adventures and Caroline talked about her day, leaving out the meeting with Rob.

When their desserts arrived, Caroline saw from the corner of her eye that someone in another booth was staring at her. It was Rob, and he was sitting next to an older man who looked to be his father, with a woman she could only assume was his mother sitting across from them.

A few moments later, he approached her table. "Well, well, well," he laughed. "Fancy seeing you here."

Caroline fidgeted in her seat, wishing he hadn't sprung himself on the two of them like that. "Hello, there. Enjoying dinner?" Caroline asked, trying to be polite.

"Yeah, with Mom and Pop. It's our weekly thing, every Saturday night."

"That's nice," Sharice replied, eyeing him. "Do we know you?"

"Oh, I apologize, ma'am. Name's Rob. I met Ms. Caroline

here earlier today and wanted to invite you both to a little get-together we're having at my dad's cabin tonight."

"We'd love to, but we can't," Sharice answered. "Early morning tomorrow, and all."

Caroline kicked her under the table. "We appreciate the invitation, Rob. Maybe another time… you know, if we ever rent the cabin again, I mean."

Rob flashed a knowing smile. "Well, I hope so. Enjoy your evening, ladies." And with that, he went back to his table.

Sharice looked at Caroline, who looked back at Sharice, but neither of them said a word.

When they were finished, the server brought the check over. "It's been paid for," she said, handing it to Sharice.

"Well, that was good of him," she said sarcastically, shooting Caroline a look of steel. They both left a generous tip before leaving the restaurant.

As they were climbing into the car, Sharice handed Caroline the receipt. "Here," she said. "I believe this was intended for you."

On the back of the check, there was a note. "682 Bluebird Lane. Rob."

"You are a grown-ass woman, C. We go way back, you and me, so you know I always tell you what I think. And I gotta say it: this is a *terrible fucking idea.*"

"I'm not gonna go, don't worry. Let's just go home," she said, squeezing Sharice's hand before turning the key in the ignition. Things had been rough with Hassan since the miscarriage, but she loved him, and she knew he loved her. And she'd never been the type to cheat.

* * *

Within 30 minutes of arriving back at the cabin, Sharice was asleep, snoring away on the couch. Caroline woke her up enough to walk her to her room.

For a few minutes, Caroline sat alone in the darkness of the living room, the fire in the hearth long burnt out. She listed in her mind all the reasons she should stay put:

It was cold out.

She loved Hassan.

It was dark.

She loved Hassan.

She was already tipsy.

She loved Hassan.

A thought occurred to her, taking her back to the night Hassan arrived. Clean and tedious in his looks as he typically was, he'd fallen out of the habit of shaving, leaving his nether regions a veritable jungle to maneuver when oral sex was the order of the day. But that evening, as he slammed hard and desperate into her, she felt the prick of fresh, coarse hairs, scratching and roughing up her own tender nether regions. He must have shaved several days ago, while he was on the trip, not that morning or even the night before.

Why would he need to shave his shaft and balls on a guys' trip? she wondered.

As she pondered, Hassan's entire story unraveled. She'd asked to see pictures of the resort, but he'd apologized, saying he'd forgotten to take any—they were just so busy having fun. So there was no proof he'd gone to Puerto Rico at all.

Moreover, Caroline had no way of knowing *who* Hassan had traveled with. She hadn't spoken to any of his friends or their wives—she hadn't ever been the type to befriend a woman just because their husbands were friends.

CHAPTER 12

So where had he been, and with whom?!

Hard as she tried to push it from her mind, her hunger for connection coupled with the flash of Rob's smile and the fear of Hassan's almost-certain betrayal all mixed together, creating a cocktail of discomfort in her belly. So against her better judgment, Caroline left a note for Sharice, slipped on her boots and coat, and began walking toward 682 Bluebird Lane.

13

Chapter 13

The path leading to Rob's cabin was lit with solar garden lights, casting a warm, inviting glow across the ground. He was sitting on the porch swing on the front deck, a can of beer in one hand and a cigarette in the other. His father sat next to him. A few other people were ambling about inside the house while gentle acoustic music played.

"Well, hello there, little missy," the old man said.

"Hello, sir. It's nice of you to invite me," Caroline answered, stepping up onto the deck.

Rob stood and took a seat in an adjacent deck chair, offering her the warm spot he'd just vacated. He put out his cigarette and waved the smoke away, apologizing.

"Is it always this beautiful at night?" Caroline asked the elder gentleman.

"Oh, yes. It can get much colder, and wetter, but this is pretty typical."

"Your friend couldn't make it?" Rob asked. "I don't think she's fond of me, much."

"Sharice isn't fond of most people. Don't take it personally," she replied.

"So what do you think of the cabin? I trust you're enjoying your stay at our Lighthouse Reach?" asked Rob's father, with a twinkle in his eye.

Of course, she thought to herself. It all made sense now.

"Wait, *you're* the owner? Mr. Harrison?"

"The one and only," he smiled, shaking her hand.

"Hey, I'm Mr. Harrison, too, Pop," Rob laughed, slapping his father on the back.

"No, you're 'Mr. Harrison, *Junior*' and you'll remain that way until I kick the bucket," he said sternly. "And I don't plan on doing *that* anytime soon!"

"Can I get you a beer?" Rob asked her.

"I had some wine with dinner, so I'm good. Otherwise, I'm not sure I'd make it back home tonight in the dark."

"Oh, Robby would help ya," Mr. Harrison replied with a smirk.

Rob turned his attention to her. "Would you like a tour of the place? Old log cabin, built in the late 1800s." Caroline's love of old books was only rivaled by her love of old houses, so she happily accepted the offer.

Mr. Harrison's cabin was much larger than the one she was renting, and it had that rustic, old cabin feel to it.

The dining room table was a long, polished wood slab. It had benches on each side and hand-made chairs at each end. While the rest of the cabin was simple and cozy, the kitchen was modernized, with stainless steel countertops and an imposing hood, as well as a rack hanging above, with various pots and pans dangling from it. Someone *clearly* enjoyed cooking in that kitchen.

All throughout the house, people chatted animatedly, and Caroline felt relieved that Rob's tour meant she didn't have to greet everyone. She liked people well enough, but having to make small talk with perfect strangers was like hot irons being poked into her eyeballs.

At the end of the tour, Rob took her upstairs to show off all the football and hockey trophies from his high school years.

"Quite the bedroom for a teenage boy," she laughed, teasing him.

"Oh, I haven't lived here in years," he remarked. "I only use the kitchen. Otherwise, I live alone in my *man lodge*, out back," he said proudly, pointing through the window to a much smaller cabin on the back edge of the property, closer to the lake.

"Oooh, a *man lodge*," Caroline laughed. "All to yourself?"

"Yep," he said. "A few tried, but no woman's been able to domesticate me yet."

Caroline chuckled and followed him out the back door.

As Robb was leading her down the steps to the squat little cabin out back, Hassan texted her. "You guys alive?"

"I am, but I can't guarantee Sharice is. Left her back at the cabin snoozing. I'm getting a local tour."

"Be careful and have fun," he texted back. "Call me later?"

"Of course."

"Everything okay?" Rob asked as they walked down to his cabin.

"Oh, yeah. Just my daughter checking in." She was getting more comfortable with lying by the minute.

"Ah, okay," he said.

Several kayaks and a few canoes were leaned up against the side of the cabin. "So... you like to row, eh?" Caroline asked.

CHAPTER 13

"Yeah, I lead a team. You can find us out here on the lake, three mornings a week." Now his ample, rippling arms and broad shoulders made sense.

He opened the door of his cabin and led her inside. The furnishings were much more sparse than in his father's cabin, and the air smelled of stale cigar smoke and a vaguely peppery cologne. A rocking chair sat in one corner next to a lamp made of tree branches. A queen-sized bed sat against the largest wall in the large central living area, with a small couch sitting against another wall. There was no TV in sight.

"Whatcha think?" he asked.

"Yeah, you weren't kidding. No female lives here," she replied, gesturing around the room. "Not a *hint* of femininity in sight."

He laughed out loud. "Like I said."

"And no TV?"

"I'd rather be outside, *living* and shit. Pops says they rot your brain, and my brain's already on its last leg."

"Do you play?" she asked, gesturing to the guitar in the corner.

He picked it up gingerly, strumming a few chords. "Not so much anymore. You?"

"I tried when I was younger, but I gave up before I could develop the callouses."

"Wimp," he laughed, setting the guitar back down.

The two of them sat on his front porch together for what felt like hours, talking about everything under the sun. By the time Caroline looked at her phone, it was nearly two o'clock in the morning.

"I should head back to the cabin," she remarked, yawning.

"Oh, yeah? I guess it's pretty late," he said, standing. "Too bad you're leaving tomorrow."

"First thing in the morning," she replied.

"Well, that's a real pity. You're gonna miss out on the gun show!" he said, flexing his biceps.

They both laughed and he took a few steps closer. This close, Caroline saw curly gray and white hairs speckling his beard.

"Hey, how old are you anyway?" Caroline asked, guilt rising higher in her throat.

"Let's agree I'm older than you."

"How old do you think I am?"

Rob chuckled to himself. "That ass ain't a day over twenty-five or I'm a monkey's uncle."

"Try adding a decade."

"I don't mind. I love me a *mature woman*," he whispered.

And there it was. If she had any doubt about his intentions, he cleared them right up. And if she were honest with herself, she knew *exactly* what she was doing, too, every step of the way. She knew what it was leading to, or could lead to, and she wanted it—not him necessarily, but the feeling of being *desired* again.

Rob stepped close enough that she could feel his breath on her cheek. She looked up into his gray eyes, and before she knew it, she was kissing him.

Tired, slightly drunk, and kissing a man she didn't know in a cabin she could barely point out on a map—none of these were the ingredients of a positively memorable experience, but she couldn't stop herself.

In no time, her shirt came off, then his pants, and soon she was down to her panties. That tiny voice in the back of her mind telling her to *run* was screaming.

CHAPTER 13

"We have to stop," she said, pushing herself away from him.

"Why?" he whispered into her neck. "You know you want this."

Sweet Jesus, she wanted it. "Because Rob. I'm married."

He stopped and looked her hard in the eyes, dramatically feigning shock and anger. "And?" he asked, dropping the facade.

"And?! I am *married*. I shouldn't be here."

He smiled and stroked the side of her face with the back of his hand. "Don't tell me you think you've found the only faithful man in America. *Come on*, Caroline. Don't be so naive. It's not a good look."

Now he'd gone too far. She couldn't stop thinking about Hassan's shaved pubes, and it enraged her, thinking Rob may be right.

"You know nothing about me, and nothing about my husband," she said, putting her clothes back on.

"Maybe not, but I can see you must be mighty dissatisfied or you wouldn't be in a stranger's cabin with your clothes off, sweetheart," he said, going in to kiss her again.

She turned away from him, toward the door. "Please, thank your father for his hospitality."

As she was reaching for the door handle, Rob stepped in front of her. "Calm down, now. Can we talk about this? I'm sorry I offended you."

She took a seat in the rocking chair next to the wood-burning stove, exhausted. It seemed the safer and smarter thing than trying to move a man twice her size. "What do you want to say?" she asked, rubbing her temples.

"Look, I'm sorry. I could sense the chemistry between us. I just wanted to enjoy some time with you while you're in town.

I'm not a home-wrecker."

"You can't wreck someone else's home without their permission," Caroline said. "Now, please move aside."

Rod sighed heavily but stepped aside. "Your loss, sweetheart."

"I am not your sweetheart," she replied, turning the door handle and stepping out into the night.

* * *

A few weeks after she returned from her trip, Caroline awoke to the familiar feeling of vomit churning in her gut. After a pregnancy test confirmed her suspicions, she thanked all the gods she hadn't given herself over to Rob.

Learning she was pregnant again was nothing like the first time. Hassan didn't pick her up and carry her around the house, crying tears of joy, and they agreed not to tell anyone.

For twenty weeks, Caroline held her breath. When they finally felt the coast was clear and told Audrey the news, she was overjoyed. She insisted on throwing the baby shower herself, inviting all her friends and even the neighbors. For the first time since the miscarriage, joy filled the air in their home.

Hassan and Caroline grew nearer, too. Somehow, even the morning sickness and endless aches and pains brought them closer. She decided there was no point in confronting him about what may or may not have happened on his "boys' trip." It was probably nothing, she reasoned with herself, so she decided instead to throw her energy into preparing for their new baby.

III

Part Three

14

Chapter 14

Jamal Hassan Soliman was born on a sweltering Tuesday night in July. Hassan missed his son's birth by 27 minutes—stuck in traffic.

From the day he was born, Jamal cried incessantly, day and night. It didn't matter what Caroline did, or what Hassan did, or what Audrey did—not even Caroline's dad could calm him during the several weeks he was in town to help. They tried all the tricks she'd learned when Audrey was a baby—long walks, nighttime drives around the block, dancing with him in a sling against her chest. But still, he screamed, his face beat-red with effort and frustration.

The doctors said it was colic, but nothing they tried seemed to give him any relief. In a last-ditch effort to avoid having to switch to formula, Caroline changed up her diet. After several weeks of trial and error, they discovered the culprit. A week or two without dairy and Jamal was like a different baby.

Hardships aside, Hassan took to fatherhood like a fish to water. Then again, having seen the way he treated Audrey, Caroline was always pretty sure he would. The two of them worked like a seasoned team, braving the early days of babyhood as best they could. They developed a rhythm of life that worked for them. There was still a shadow of grief hanging over their marriage, but they had come to a peaceful meeting place, and all seemed well.

* * *

A few days shy of Jamal's first birthday, Hassan's mother received devastating news—stage four colon cancer. She'd been struggling for months but had kept it to herself, and now it was too late for chemo to do much of anything, aside from draining her of her last remaining energy.

She'd elected to spend her last days in Cairo, where she'd been placed in hospice care. Her doctors said she wouldn't make it to the end of the month. There was no choice for Hassan and his siblings but to go be with her.

"I'll be home within the month," he promised.

"There's no rush, *habibi*," Caroline replied. "Be with your mama and your family. And please extend our apologies. We wish we could come, but Jamal is still too small."

"No, of course not. They will understand," he assured her.

But there were deeper reasons he knew nothing of: Caroline hadn't the slightest clue what was expected of her in their culture, as far as death and dying. She worried she'd get in the way more than she'd be of any help. And with the energy it took to care for an infant and an increasingly moody teenager, she was spent.

The three of them went with Hassan to the airport and saw him off. He held Jamal tight and kissed his forehead three

CHAPTER 14

times, reciting an Arabic prayer. He hugged Audrey and kissed Caroline sweetly, lingering longer than he typically would have in public, then turned and walked through the gate to the security area.

* * *

Hassan texted her some twelve hours later to tell her he'd arrived. Then he was radio silent for several days.

Caroline feared the worst—that his mother had already passed and he was wrapped up in the funeral arrangements and details—but tried to be patient and calm as she waited.

Finally, a week later, he called her on video. His eyes were rimmed with dark circles. People were crying in the background, so Caroline decided against inviting Audrey in to talk with him.

"Hassan, are you okay? How is your mom?" Caroline asked.

"She's fading. It's..." he choked up, "Caroline, it's the most horrible suffering, watching her like this. She's a corpse, a barely breathing corpse, and she's in so much pain and..."

Caroline was quiet for a minute, giving him space to express his feelings if he needed to, but he just wept.

"Where's Audrey? How are you guys? Is Jamal sleeping better?" he asked, rapid-fire, wiping his eyes.

"She's out with friends," Caroline lied. "And I've just put Jamal down for his nap, too. He was nursing like crazy today. He's about to have another growth spurt."

"That's good to hear," Hassan said, smiling. "And how are you, *habibti*? I've missed you so much. It's been hard to get away and make a call."

"I'm holding up okay, I suppose," she said. "Jamal's colic is much better now, so that's good. And Audrey is less... Audrey lately, I guess."

"No, baby. How are *you*?"

She took a deep breath. It had been quite a while since anyone asked how *she* was doing and meant it. Ever since Jamal was born, everyone was so focused on how the baby was doing, how he was sleeping, eating, shitting, teething, growing. She had very little energy left to assess how *she* was doing.

"I miss you so much. It's hard without you," she said. "I can't believe it's only been a week."

"I can't wait to have you near me again. You and our babies."

Caroline smiled but wanted to return to the point at hand. "Tell me, Hassan. What do they say about your mama?"

Hassan stepped out onto a balcony for more privacy. The familiar sounds of Cairo traffic blared in the background. "It's not good, Lina. She has a week, at most. It's... scary," he said, choking up again.

"How are the girls holding up? And Majed?" she asked. "And did your father arrive yet?"

"Everyone is holding it together as best they can. Baba had some sort of hold-up at the airport, something about his Egyptian passport. But he should be here tomorrow, *inshaAllah*."

Jamal whimpered from his crib across the room, so Caroline excused herself to pick him up.

When Hassan saw his son on camera, he smiled big. "*Habibi* Jamal, Baba's joy! I miss you, my love," he said.

They sat like this for some time, not saying much, until someone stepped out on the balcony to bring Hassan back in.

"Let's talk in a few days, okay, *habibti*?"

"Of course."

"I love you," he said. "Tell Audrey I love her, too, and kiss Jamal for Baba."

"We love you, too," she said before the call ended.

Chapter 15

In light of Hassan's mother's illness, Caroline was overcome with a desire to spend time with her last remaining parent. So she booked a flight to visit her father in Indiana.

The old farmhouse at the end of the long drive looked almost exactly like it had all her life, albeit a bit updated. Her father, Charlie, had installed solar panels on both the house and the barn roofs, and invested in red aluminum siding.

Charlie stepped out onto the covered porch and took off his hat and squinted to see who was coming. A grin spread across his face when he realized it was her. Behind him ran his old golden retriever, Larry, thrilled to have visitors.

"What a welcome surprise, darlin'!" he said, throwing his arms around Caroline when she got out of the car. He smelled of shaving cream and leather, like he always had. *Home.*

"Sorry I didn't warn you I was coming. It was sort of... last minute."

Charlie shrugged it off. "This is your *home*, silly. You don't gotta tell me when you're coming," he said, opening the back

CHAPTER 15

door where Jamal was sitting. "How did this little stinker get so big so damn fast?" he asked, unbuckling Jamal. "I bet you can run like the wind, little man!"

Jamal sat in his car seat, staring up at Charlie as he unbuckled him and picked him up.

"Looks nothing like you," Charlie added. "Good for him!"

Caroline laughed and took Jamal from him.

Audrey nearly jumped into Charlie's arms once they were free. "Grandpappy!" she squealed, and she was five years old again, all glee.

"I'm so glad to see you, kiddo!" Charlie laughed, hugging Audrey tight. "Let's get you guys inside. It's hotter than hell out here," he said, picking up their bags and ushering them inside.

The interior of the house was largely unchanged, too. Charlie, like Caroline, was a creature of habit, resistant to unnecessary change—and even some necessary ones. Whenever Mimi came to visit, she complained about the dated decor, but Caroline found it soothing. It was something sure, something she could come back to for comfort when the breakneck pace of L.A. became too much.

After they'd gotten settled in, Caroline grabbed a few carrots from the fridge and slipped on some old work boots from the back porch. "I'm gonna go see Nelly," she said, heading out the back door.

"Be careful, she gets spooked easily these days," Charlie called after her.

"Got it."

When Caroline was a child, Charlie used to raise pigs, chickens, and goats. But he'd sold the animals years ago. Now, he and his crew worked hard year after year, planting, raising, and harvesting corn and soybeans to sell for a profit to the government.

Charlie had kept Nelly out of sentiment. She was only a foal when Caroline's mother died, and they'd had her mother Bertha for years before that. At her old age, Nelly spent her days grazing lazily across her domain and being coddled by Charlie and the vets and caretakers he still paid to look after her.

Caroline stepped into the old barn. It was now a machine shop, full of tractors and field farm equipment in various stages of disrepair—all but the far southern corner, where Nelly's stall stood, marked by the sign above the stall that Caroline had made with a wood-burning set she'd gotten for a Christmas gift one year.

When Caroline approached her, Nelly shuffled her feet and flared her nostrils.

"It's just me, old girl," Caroline said, grabbing the carrot from her back pocket and reaching through the fence. When Nelly smelled the carrot, she relaxed a little. "Yeah, I know. It's been a while," Caroline said, letting Nelly sniff her hand. "I'm sorry I have been away so long. Life happened."

Nelly gobbled up the carrot and whinnied happily, moving her snout near so Caroline could rub it.

* * *

After that first encounter, things were easier between them. Eventually, Caroline was able to saddle Nelly and take her for a slow trot around the yard. Soon, Caroline made a ritual of

CHAPTER 15

it, starting each day with a ride. She found herself relaxing for the first time in a long time.

When she wasn't riding Nelly, Caroline and Audrey helped Charlie and the farm hands with the chores. Audrey was so happy with her Grandpappy that she let down her teenage angst. Caroline hadn't seen her that happy in years. Jamal, too, made himself at home. He bounced and giggled and held his arms out to his grandfather anytime he toddled into a room and saw Charlie there.

In the evenings, Charlie would teach Audrey how to cook old family favorites. After dinner, the four of them would sit enjoying the cool night breeze and listening to the crickets and cicadas singing. It felt so good to just *be* there—no expectations, no fear of the future, and no regret over the past.

Though she'd intended to stay for a few days, time flew by and Caroline found herself unable to peel away just yet. Before she knew it, two weeks had passed, and she had no desire to go elsewhere.

* * *

One afternoon, Caroline sat smoking on the front porch as summer rain thundered overhead on the roof—one of her favorite sounds. Her father came out of the screen door and sat in his old rocking chair next to her, sipping sweet iced tea. Larry the dog joined the party, nudging Caroline's hand for head rubs.

"Heard from Hassan, yet?" Charlie asked. He knew she was worried by the way her eyebrows were knit together—the way they always were when something was bothering her, even when she was little.

Caroline shook her head and took a drag off her cigarette, petting away at Larry's head. "No. I know he's dealing with a lot, though, so I'm not surprised."

"I understand grief, better than most. But he left my baby and her babies alone for weeks, and he barely says a word. Do the phones not work over there in the Middle East? Come on, now."

"I dunno, Dad. There's no point in harassing him about it, though."

Charlie made a sound of recognition and looked out across the land. "I suppose."

The two of them sat in silence for a beat.

"I gotta tell you, Audrey is becoming such a splendid young lady," he said. "Reminds me of your mother when she was young."

Caroline smiled, turning toward him and putting her cigarette out in the tray. "Tell me more about what she was like when she was younger?"

So Charlie regaled her with stories about her mother—about their love, about their tough times. He even told her the story about when they lost Mimi at an amusement park—a story Caroline had heard a hundred times, but never tired of hearing. That was the summer before her mom died.

"I remember so little about her, really," Caroline said. "I know I was only seven when she passed, but I feel like I should remember more. Mostly I remember her laugh… and her hands, odd as that is."

Caroline's father took a deep breath. "She really did have the most beautiful hands. And don't feel bad. The mind does funny things to protect us from pain, Caroline," he said, patting her hand. "Your mother was a troubled woman, to be sure, and times weren't always pleasant. But she loved us all so much. I can tell you that for certain."

Jamal appeared behind the screen door, whining and rubbing his eyes, having awoken from his afternoon nap. Caroline stood to grab him, but when he saw Charlie, he reached toward him instead.

"That's right, come to Grandpappy," Charlie said, standing to go get Jamal. The two of them sat together, rocking in his chair while Charlie patted Jamal's back until he fell asleep again on his shoulder.

"Do you ever wish you'd had a son?" Caroline asked her father.

"Oh, no. Nope. Your sister was all the boy we could ever need, what with all her trouble-making and shenanigans." Both of them laughed. "And she's one hell of a hunter, too. Makes me proud."

"Hey, we can't all be Mimi, Daddy," Caroline laughed.

"You make me proud in your own ways, darlin'" he smiled.

Audrey walked out of the screen door, headphones on and hood down.

"I think I'll get going on dinner," Charlie remarked, carrying Jamal in and rubbing Audrey's head as he passed her.

Audrey took a seat on a deck chair next to her mother, saying nothing and staring out at the cornfields. Larry trotted over to Audrey, apparently finished with Caroline now that Audrey had arrived.

"Hey there, kid," Caroline said.

Audrey nodded in her direction, then went back to staring out at the fields with her headphones on. The two of them had grown distant with Jamal's arrival, but Caroline knew her baby was still in there somewhere.

"How's it going?" Caroline asked Audrey.

"Good."

"You need anything?"

"I wish I could talk to Hassan," Audrey said, keeping her eyes trained on the horizon. The sky was a vivid display of pastel pinks and baby blues.

"I dunno if he's up for much in the way of conversation these days. But I'll text him for you."

"No need. I already did. I think his phone is off or something."

"Maybe."

"When is he coming home, Mom? Is he okay?"

"I'm not sure, honey. But yes, he will be okay, in time."

"Are you sure? His mom is dying, Mom. I would *not* be okay if you died, not ever. When you die, I mean…"

Caroline reached out and took Audrey's hand in hers. "That won't happen for a long time. Don't worry. And Hassan will be home soon. It'll all be okay."

"I guess," Audrey said, rubbing Larry with her free hand.

* * *

After a full month in Indiana, Caroline and Audrey were ready to get back to their lives in L.A.

Caroline's father helped them load up the car. "When you talk to Hassan, give him my condolences, and tell him he's due for a trip out here to visit his father-in-law," Charlie said, hugging them all tight.

"Will do, Daddy," Caroline replied, saluting him and getting

CHAPTER 15

into the driver's seat.

"And you, Ms. Audrey," Charlie said, leaning in to the passenger window, "You'd better call your Grandpappy more, okay? Don't make me come out there and give you the what-for."

Audrey laughed and kissed her Grandpappy on the cheek. "Yes, sir!"

16

Chapter 16

Hassan's mother died on a Friday morning in late August—a fact Caroline learned from his family's posts on social media. No matter how many times she texted and called Hassan, he never answered, and her messages to his family went unread.

Then, a week after his mother passed, Hassan showed up unannounced—a full 30 pounds lighter, looking like he'd been on a bender for a month. He took a shower and went straight to bed, and he did not leave their room for a week.

When he finally climbed out of bed, he began praying the *salat* for the first time since they'd met. Five times a day, every day, he would make a wet mess of the bathroom floor, washing his hands, face, arms, head, and feet. Then he'd roll out the intricately woven carpet he had brought home from Egypt, announce the call to prayer, recite the prescribed words in Arabic, and perform the ritual movements.

Caroline chalked it all up to grief—something she was intimately familiar with—but as the weeks turned to months, he became more and more intense in his devotion.

CHAPTER 16

The first thing to go was alcohol. He came home from work one day and poured every last drop of it down the drain. Of course, she always found a place to hide her wine bottles here and there, but when Hassan would find one, they'd get into heated arguments that could last for days.

"This is *my house*," he would say, "and I will be held responsible for the sin that happens in it."

"I am *not Muslim*, Hassan, and I never agreed to abide by these rules," Caroline would say in defense. "And this is *our* house, not yours. What on earth has gotten into you?!"

At that point, Hassan would curse in Arabic under his breath and stomp away, and that was the end of the conversation, until the next time he caught her drinking—and he always caught her, eventually. Hassan's anger only seemed to increase her drinking. The secrecy and shame and fear that he would find out somehow made it even harder to resist.

Hassan even gave up the music he previously loved. Instead of playing Umm Kulthum songs every morning while they drank their coffee like he had since the first night they spent together, he started playing long, mournful Quran recitations.

He also started taking Fridays off, insisting it was a day for rest and family and community. He took Jamal with him to the mosque and showed him off to the men there, and he started trying to teach him how to pray. He even convinced Caroline and Audrey to attend one Friday.

Though Caroline tried to maintain an open mind, she struggled. The extreme segregation of men and women and the cold response from the people she met there—plus, the fact that most of them didn't speak English—made them feel unwelcome and alien. Plus, the imam spoke at length about the importance of women dressing modestly to "protect the souls of the men"—as if it was a woman's responsibility if a man lusted after her, something even Audrey knew was absurd. So they never went back.

Oddly, Hassan was hornier than ever. He would pull Caroline into bed daily and take his time with her, ensuring she was fully pleased before allowing himself to climax. On the one hand, Caroline was grateful that he had reverted to the way he had been at the beginning of their relationship, at least when it came to his concern for her pleasure. She welcomed the chance for intimacy with him—or something like it—but it was an odd change, contradicted by so many other odd changes since he came home from Egypt.

Caroline watched all these changes taking place and wrung her hands in helplessness. She worried that if she said anything, it would set him off, and she had no idea how this new version of Hassan would react.

So she wore noise-canceling headphones when he played his Qur'an recitations on full blast, continued to conceal her drinking habit, and made her best effort to patiently wait and observe what would happen.

* * *

A few months after Hassan came home from Egypt, Caroline's patience seemed to have paid off.

She came home from a meeting with her editor one day to find that Hassan had returned—*her* Hassan. He'd shaved his scraggly, overgrown beard, gotten a new haircut, and was playing loud Arabic music and dancing.

He kissed her passionately when she came in, and she tasted

alcohol on his lips. "I scored a huge account at work!" he said, handing her a glass of her favorite wine. "Let's celebrate!"

"But you said—" Caroline began.

"Drink, baby!"

And just like that, Hassan's ultra-religious phase ended without so much as an explanation. He put the prayer rug in a storage bin in the basement, stopped attending the mosque, and went back to sleeping with Caroline once a week, at best.

She wasn't sure whether to laugh or cry.

Chapter 17

It was a long, lonely winter. Hassan had thrown himself back into his work, like nothing ever happened, and Audrey was busy with her friends, as always. Maria had moved to San Diego and Nikki was wrapped up in dealing with Maya's teenage dramas. Even Sharice was unavailable, caught up in making wedding plans with Jayden.

So, Jamal, the TV, and several glasses of wine a night kept Caroline company through the dark and lonely winter months and into the first vestiges of Spring.

Though she usually found the winter months to be a wonderfully inspiring time, Caroline rarely wrote that year, claiming she had a bad case of writer's block. In truth, the combination of alcohol and the almost complete lack of baby-free time meant she rarely had enough functional brain cells to generate a full grocery list, let alone literary magic from thin air.

To make matters worse, the gulf that had opened between Caroline and Audrey only widened with each season that passed. Audrey had moved beyond her angsty, emo stage and into her full-blown cute girl stage, and Caroline was terrified.

CHAPTER 17

Thinking of her own premature entrance into the world of sex and desire, Caroline recalled it was neither pleasant nor entirely consensual. So the more Audrey tried to find her autonomy, the more Caroline held on. The more Audrey begged for freedom, the tighter Caroline pulled on her leash. She knew it wasn't a sustainable relationship pattern.

One Friday evening, shortly after Audrey's 15th birthday, Caroline sat relaxing with yet another glass of wine while Jamal slept when there were three loud knocks at the door. Hassan was out of town for business, yet again, and Audrey was watching a movie at her friend Lauren's house, so Caroline had no idea who it could be.

When she opened the front door, a police officer greeted her, alongside Audrey, who hung her head in shame.

"Ma'am, your daughter and several other teenagers were pulled over this evening. The driver was drunk. I didn't give your daughter a breathalyzer test, but she's obviously intoxicated," the officer said.

"Thank you for bringing her home, sir," Caroline said. "I assure you, this is a 'first and *only* time' sort of situation."

"I'm sure it is, ma'am," he said, walking back to his cruiser.

"Where's Lauren?" Caroline asked him.

"They booked her in," the officer replied as he climbed into his car and drove away.

Caroline closed the door and turned to her daughter. "Audrey..." she started.

"I know, Mom. Just... don't tell Hassan, please. Let me talk to him."

"Audrey, this isn't about Hassan or how he will react. This is about you lying to me. Why didn't you tell me what you'd be doing tonight?"

"Really, Mom? *Now?*" Audrey sighed and took a seat at the kitchen table.

"Yes, really. You told me you were gonna hang at Lauren's house."

"We *were* at Lauren's house, I swear," she started. "But then some guys came over with beer and they wanted to go to the beach. Lauren drove because I don't have my license yet. She didn't *seem* that drunk..." Audrey stopped when she saw the look on her mother's face. "Please, Mom. Don't look at me like that."

"Audrey—"

"*You* are hardly one to judge in this scenario, Mrs. 'I drink alone every night.'"

Caroline was sad earlier, but now she was plain angry. *How dare she?* "*I* am an adult, Audrey. And this isn't about me."

"Yes, Mom. You *are* an adult, and you drink like a fish," she said. "How do you expect me to handle my pain when you can't even handle your perfect life without an entire fucking bottle of wine every night?"

"Language, Audrey," Caroline said. Because there wasn't much else she *could* say—not from her glass house with her handful of pebbles. "Please, take a shower and head to bed. We will talk about this more in the morning."

Alone in the living room, Caroline sat on the couch, holding her face in her hands. Audrey's words echoed through her mind: *How do you expect me to handle my pain when you can't even handle your perfect life without an entire fucking bottle of wine every night?*

What pain? There was clearly more to her daughter's life than Caroline knew. But then, Audrey was right about her drinking problem. How could she possibly keep up with her

CHAPTER 17

daughter if she spent nearly every evening drowning in a glass of wine?

On that note, how much of the distance between her and Hassan could also be blamed on her drinking habit? It was a classic chicken-or-egg scenario: was Hassan away all the time, never available when she needed him, cold and distant until he wanted sex *because* Caroline was at least a little tipsy every night? Or was Caroline drowning her loneliness and insecurities in a glass or two of wine every night *because* her husband was completely unavailable in every sense of the word?

Her knee-jerk reaction was to grab a bottle of wine and pop it open to help ease the worry and sadness she felt rolling over her.

Yep, she thought. *I'm a goddamned alcoholic.*

So Caroline turned off the TV, poured out the rest of her wine, and climbed into bed. She lay there for what felt like hours, staring up at the ceiling—not reading, not snacking, not scrolling mindlessly through her phone. For once, she just sat with her feelings, letting the fear and worry wash over her as she wept into her hands. Eventually, she fell asleep right there on top of her blankets.

* * *

Caroline awoke the next morning to a text from Hassan, saying he would be home by dinner. The meeting was going longer than he anticipated. *Of course it was.*

Rather than wallowing in the obsessive insecurities and jealousies that usually occupied her mind when these moments happened, Caroline decided to spend some time with Audrey.

"Let's head to the mall and get our nails done," she said when Audrey cracked open her bedroom door.

Audrey hesitated, confused. "You... aren't *punishing* me?"

"My mistake. I was sure the *last* thing you'd want to do this morning is chill with your lame mom," Caroline laughed.

"Touche," Audrey said, chuckling and closing her door to get dressed.

Caroline got Jamal washed and dressed and dropped him off with Harley, the college student she had hired to babysit him on occasion, and then she headed to the mall with Audrey.

They wandered from shop to shop for hours. Caroline bought Audrey several new outfits and they found a new nail place and got their nails done. Caroline kept their conversation light and fun until, over lunch, she decided it was time to address the elephant in the room.

"So... about last night..." Caroline started.

Audrey took a deep breath. "Yeah?"

"Calm down, it's not a lecture."

"Oh?" Audrey said, relaxing.

"I wanted to ask about the pain you mentioned. What's wrong, kid? Just normal life stuff, or is there something more?"

Audrey gazed down at her burger and took a drink of her milkshake. "I mean... it's that, yeah. But it's more. I just... don't feel like I *belong* anywhere, Mom."

"Hey, we've all felt that way," Caroline said, leaning forward and lowering her voice. "I guarantee every other kid in your class feels like that or has before."

"I know I'm nothing special..." Audrey said, trailing off.

Caroline took Audrey's hand and rubbed it between her own. "That's not what I meant, honey. Of course, your experience is your own. I only meant you're not alone."

Audrey nodded.

"But if there's something else bothering you, you can tell me. I may struggle to handle my own 'perfect life' but I do have *some* wisdom to offer, sometimes."

"Well..." Audrey began, anxiously pushing her hair behind her ears.

"Yeah?"

"So something happened a few months ago and I haven't talked with you about it because I wasn't sure what to say."

Caroline felt a chill creeping up her spine. "Audrey, did someone... *hurt you?*"

"What? Mom... what?! No! I mean, I get why you'd jump to that conclusion. But no, it's nothing like that."

Now it was Caroline who needed a deep breath. "Okay, good. Thanks for clearing the air on that one," she said. "We've always taught you about your right to bodily autonomy, and good touch, bad touch, and all that, so I hoped it was nothing like *that*."

"Of course, Mom. No. I would tell you right away if anything like that ever happened," she said.

"So, what is it?"

Audrey laid her head back on the top of the chair. "I... I don't think I'm *normal*. Like... sexually," she said.

"Being straight isn't *normal* if that's what you mean."

"No, I don't mean... I'm saying I like all types of people, and it doesn't really matter what their gender is. I like what I like... I dunno. Do you think I'm weird?" She looked at Caroline's face, waiting for her response.

Caroline could see the fear in her daughter's eyes. "You're my baby. All I want for you is to be loved, as you are, and treated with respect," Caroline said. "And I don't care who it is, or what their gender is. I just want to see you loved and cared for."

Audrey began to tear up.

"Have you spoken with Lauren or any of your other friends about it?" Caroline asked.

Audrey looked mortified. "No, Mom! Never. Oh my god, they'd think I was a freak. I'd never be invited anywhere again. They already make fun of me because I've never been kissed. I can't afford to lose my friends."

"Oh, Audrey. I'm so sorry. But baby a true friend would *never* walk out on you like that or make fun of you for who you love or feel attracted to."

Audrey chuckled. "Yeah."

"I mean it."

"Well anyway," Audrey said, playing with the napkin. "That's the pain I was talking about, the reason I drink with Lauren sometimes," she said, looking ashamed. "That and like… everything else about being a teenager at the end of the world."

"I understand," Caroline replied. "And as we've established, I'm not one to talk. But drinking or drug use are *not* healthy ways to cope with your pain."

"It's *so hard*, though, Mom," she said, as tears began falling down her cheeks. "I don't want to be alone forever. I want to find love, but I can't be anything other than what I am, and I've never met anyone like me. I know you can't understand."

Caroline looked out at the food court, pondering how to respond. "What you're dealing with is a particular kind of pain I can't relate to. That's true. But I'm still here for you. I *will* listen and try my hardest to understand," Caroline assured her. "And we are *both* going to do some work on managing our pain better. I'm gonna call some therapists on Monday, okay?"

"Thanks, Mom," Audrey said, drying her tears. "And... I'm sorry about what I said last night."

"I know you said what you said last night to hurt me, but it's true," Caroline said, looking down at her hands. "I *do* have a problem, and I'm gonna work on it."

"I believe in you," Audrey said, beaming.

Caroline smiled. Audrey had always been a goodhearted kid, and though things had gotten much harder in her teen years, Caroline was so proud of the person Audrey was becoming.

"We'd better get going. It's time to pick up Jamal," Caroline said, glancing down at her watch. "Plus, Hassan will be home tonight. We gotta get the house ready."

"Hey so... am I in trouble, for last night?" Audrey asked as she started cleaning up the table.

Caroline sat for a second, thinking about how best to handle things. "We should talk with Hassan, together."

"Okay. But let me be the one to tell him about... my sexuality."

"Of course. That's your story to tell, whenever you're ready."

* * *

A few weeks later, Caroline was sitting at her computer one morning, working away on the final edits for a screenplay she'd been struggling with, when she received an email notification.

"They want it! They want 'The Frenzy of Life'! Check it out!" her agent, Greta, had written. Below, Caroline read the forwarded email.

Dear Greta and Caroline,

We enjoyed reading this screenplay! We'd love to invite you both into the office this week to discuss the possibilities. We have a few options in mind for producers who may be interested.

Caroline couldn't believe it. Greta had sent the screenplay to several producers more than six months ago and most had turned it down outright. Apparently, few were interested in producing a movie about two women who travel to the future and find the world a bleak wasteland, then fall in love and build a commune with the only remaining humans on Earth.

Well, now someone had bitten.

"Yes!" she quickly wrote back to Greta. "I'm in!"

18

Chapter 18

FIVE YEARS LATER

"Go, Jamal!" Caroline screamed. "You're almost there!" The air was thick with chlorine and anticipation as Jamal and the other boys hurtled through the water. Caroline's eyes followed his every stroke, her hands clasped tightly in her lap. Hassan sat next to her, rooting for him.

Even at such a young age, Jamal was a great swimmer—had been since Caroline took him to his first swimming lesson when he was still a toddler—but the competition that day was fierce. Jamal touched the wall mere seconds after the kid next to him, his chest heaving as he looked up at the scoreboard. Disappointment washed over his face.

Caroline and Hassan met Jamal as he climbed out of the pool.

"I lost," he mumbled, his voice barely above a whisper. His

eyes were brimming with tears, his lower lip quivering.

Hassan knelt down, bringing himself to Jamal's eye level. "You swam so well, *habibi*. We're so proud of you!"

"That's right. And you finished, baby! That's not a small thing," Caroline said, smiling, as she handed him his towel and pulled him in for a hug. "We just have to work on shaving a few seconds off your butterfly stroke and you'll be set."

"How about some ice cream on the way home?" Hassan suggested as they followed Jamal to the locker room door.

Jamal nodded, a smile breaking through his disappointment. "I guess," he said, sniffling.

* * *

When they arrived home later that afternoon, Jamal headed to the shower and then collapsed in bed, exhausted. Audrey was out with some friends and Hassan had gone to the gym, so Caroline decided to take advantage of the time alone to get some writing done and enjoy a glass of wine.

Caroline had tried to get sober after her conversation with Audrey, she really had. But every time she would get a few months of sobriety under her belt, something would go terribly wrong—or terribly *right*—and she'd be back on the bottle.

On the bright side, she'd finally developed a writing routine after years of struggling to stay on track. When she was ready to write, she'd head into her office, close the door, light a candle, turn on some music—whatever inspired the type of writing she was working on that day—and then, of course, pour herself a large glass of wine. This little ritual helped coax out the artist in her and she looked forward to it, in some ways even more than the actual writing.

And so that's what she did that night, while the summer heat gave way to the cool of the evening outside her windows. Lost in the world she was spinning on the page, she didn't hear Hassan come in until he was standing directly beside her.

"Holy shit!" she cried, removing her noise-canceling headphones and clutching her chest. "You scared the hell outta me!"

"I called your name several times," Hassan said blithely, sitting in the reading chair in the corner. "What if I'd been a burglar? Or what if Jamal needed you, huh?"

Caroline rolled her eyes and poured the rest of the wine into her glass. "Don't be dramatic. He's seven, not two. And he was sleeping anyway."

"Mm-hmm," Hassan said. He stood and perused the books on her bookshelf. He turned back toward her like he wanted to say something, but seemed to change his mind.

"Did you need something?" Caroline asked him.

"Nope. Just… letting you know I was home. I'm gonna jump in the shower. Maybe we could watch a movie or something afterward?"

Caroline knew what Hassan was hinting at. It had been weeks since they'd made love, and much as she needed a good fuck, her skin recoiled from his touch.

She'd learned to make do with sneaking her vibrator into the shower. It was faster than waiting for Hassan to get hard, and then waiting more for him to even attempt to help her orgasm.

"I wish I could," she said, "but I have this deadline tomorrow, and—"

"And we mustn't make Greta wait," Hassan said bitterly

before stepping out of the room and slamming the door behind him.

Caroline sat for a moment, unsure how to respond. It seemed like the harder she worked and the more success she garnered, the less happy Hassan was. She thought about confronting him on the matter but felt like it was pointless. He lacked the self-awareness to tell her why he did the things he did, even if she could get him to listen.

So she didn't waste her breath. She took one last sip of her wine, put her headphones back on, and fell back into the artistic hole she had been happily clamoring around in before Hassan interrupted her.

* * *

Two hours later, Jamal was the one to interrupt.

"Mom?" he said, rubbing his eyes groggily.

Caroline smiled, closing her computer. She had made excellent headway and come to a natural stopping point, and anyway, the wine was making her head swim in a pleasant, heavy sort of way. She was happy for the break.

"How was your nap?" she asked.

"It was good," he said, yawning. "You working on the one about the father who disappears in a snowstorm and then shows up on Christmas five years later?"

Caroline laughed. "Yep, that's the one."

Jamal was always so curious about her work, poking his little head in her office now and then when she was typing away. When he was smaller, he used to climb onto her lap and sit with her while she read her sentences aloud to him, skipping over

CHAPTER 18

the saucier parts. Audrey had never been much of a reader, so Caroline reveled in the joy of sharing these moments with Jamal.

"Well, I'll watch it with you when it comes out," Jamal said, coming toward her for a hug.

Caroline took him in her arms and squeezed him tight. "You sweetie," she said.

"What's for dinner?" he asked. "My tummy's rumbling."

"Let's see what we can find," Caroline said. She stood, blew out the candle, turned off the table lamp, picked up her empty wineglass, and shut the office door behind her.

* * *

Audrey was in her junior year at UCLA, working hard on her degree in International Economics. She'd elected to live at home, allowing Caroline to spend more time with her before she was finally ready to leave the nest, so it was a win-win for them both.

One morning in the fall, Audrey had an interview for a job at the library, so Caroline dropped her off and headed to a coffee shop to get some writing done.

Once Caroline had her coffee and bagel with cream cheese, she sat in a booth and began setting up her laptop and writing station. That's when she noticed a woman staring at her from the corner of her eye.

"I'm sorry, I don't mean to be rude," the woman said, coming to sit at Caroline's table. "But you are *gorgeous*."

"Thank you," Caroline replied, smiling awkwardly. She recognized the woman but couldn't place her. "Have we met?"

"No, not yet. But our sons are on the same swim team and I've seen you around, you and your partner. And I've been *dying* to ask... what do you do to your hair to get it to shine like that?!"

"Argan oil, once a week," Caroline said, smiling. It had been a while since someone noticed. "Are you Benton's mom? Jamal loves him!" With her sharp green eyes and long, dark hair, she looked like she'd wandered out of a fairy wood—just like Benton.

"Yep! I'm Shannon," she said in a bubbly voice, extending her hand to Caroline's. Caroline noted how smooth her skin was and the firmness of her handshake.

"Caroline," she replied, closing her laptop and sliding it back into the case.

"Oh, no, I didn't mean to interrupt!" Shannon exclaimed. "I just wanted to introduce myself and ask if we could arrange a play date for the boys sometime soon."

"Yes! Let's do that," Caroline said, opening the calendar app on her phone. "How does next Friday evening sound? We're having a little cookout at our house. We'd love for you all to come."

"Perfect!" Shannon said, picking up her bag and purse. "Can I get your number?"

Caroline smiled. "Sure!"

Shannon took the slip of paper from Caroline and dropped it into her purse, put her sunglasses on, and waved goodbye as she headed out to her car.

Chapter 19

On Friday night, Shannon and her husband, Ryan, showed up with their three kids in tow. In her arms, Shannon carried an enormous wicker basket, overflowing with various housewarming gifts, including a Charcuterie board with all the fixings and a bottle of wine.

While Caroline and Shannon busied themselves in the kitchen, setting everything up, Hassan and Ryan made fast work of the fire. Before long, there was a blazing bonfire in the backyard. Afterward, they sat chit-chatting while they helped the kids slide hot dogs and marshmallows onto their roasting sticks.

"They seem to be getting along," Caroline said as she emptied potato chips into bowls and Shannon poured them two glasses of wine from the bottle she'd gifted to Caroline.

"Yeah, Ryan's a nice guy," Shannon said, "if a little standoffish. Nothing like *your* husband!"

"Yeah, Hassan's definitely more outgoing than I am," Caroline said, taking a sip of the wine. It was much finer than she could afford. She savored the taste as it spread across her tongue.

"How did the two of you meet?" Shannon asked as they set out plates and cups for the kids. "It must be quite the story!"

"Oh, nothing very interesting. We met at a party," Caroline said.

Shannon frowned, disappointed with Caroline's lack of detail. "What does he do for a living?"

"He works in logistics and international shipping, that sorta thing. He works for his dad's business in Kansas City, so he travels a lot. What about Ryan?"

"What is it with men working for their dads?" Shannon said, laughing. "Ryan does too. He works for his dad's IT business. So he does a little of this and that, whatever they tell him to do. And he makes far less than he deserves."

"Yeah, it's hard when the people we love tolerate less than they deserve, for sure."

"He's a *doormat*," Shannon whispered. "But it's fine. I make more than enough money for the both of us." Noticing the look of discomfort on Caroline's face, Shannon cleared her throat and changed the subject. "So! Tell me more about you! Do you have any family nearby?"

"Nope. I'm from Indiana, so it's just me here. My sister, Mimi, comes to visit pretty often, though."

"Oh, that's gotta be so lonely! What about your husband? What's his family like?"

"They're kind enough," Caroline answered, inviting Shannon to come sit in the living room. "His dad has come here a few times and we've gone to visit him. But the rest of his family lives in Cairo part of the year, so we don't see them often."

Shannon's eyes grew wide. "Yeah? How did they treat you? Since you're not Arab, or like Middle Eastern, or whatever?

CHAPTER 19

Muslim, anyway... that's what I mean."

Caroline took a sip of wine, remembering the conversation she overheard that night on the cruise ship. "I mean... I think they *preferred* he marry someone from his own culture, but they were happy to welcome me and Audrey into the family, anyway."

"I see," Shannon said, taking a sip of her wine. "So Audrey isn't his daughter, then? I mean, I suspected as much. Look at those big blue eyes she has!"

Caroline began to feel like she was being interrogated, but she often felt that way whenever she talked to extroverts. Left to her own devices, she would tell no one anything about herself. Over time, though, she'd learned the hard way that refusing to divulge any information at all about oneself made it hard to make friends.

"Her father died when she was a baby," Caroline replied. "But she and Hassan are best buds, and have been since day one."

"Interesting!" Shannon said. "From what I understand, that's not very common over there, a man marrying a woman with kids already. Most of those guys would *never*."

"Oh, do you know many Egyptians?"

"Not Egyptians, no," Shannon said, smiling and leaning in closer. "But I have had my fair share of experiences with men from all over that part of the world."

Caroline began to understand. Maybe Shannon was once one of those women Hassan had joked about so long ago—the white women who sleep with Muslim men and think covering their heads and learning a few words in Arabic or Farsi or Persian makes them exotic and unique.

"Oh?" she asked.

Shannon giggled and took another sip of wine, leaning her

head back against the sofa. "Mm-hmm. But that was *a lifetime* ago. Way before the kids were born."

"How long have you and Ryan been married? You seem to be great together."

"We were college sweethearts," Shannon said, looking outside at her husband. "But that was ages ago, too. We've grown apart, I guess. We're *very* different people than we were back then, I'll put it like that. But, anyway, enough about me and my crazy life! Let's go check on the kids."

With that, they set their empty wine glasses in the sink and headed outside.

* * *

After that first meeting, Caroline and Shannon were inseparable. Though they couldn't have been more different from one another, they found a connection in their shared fascination with studying world religions and foreign cultures.

Caroline found Shannon interesting. The youngest child of a wealthy entrepreneur and a devoted stay-at-home mother, Shannon had lived a life of relative ease. She regaled Caroline with stories of her family's travels around the world, of their stays at Martha's Vineyard, and their annual trips to Europe. Compared to Caroline's humble upbringing, Shannon's life seemed like a movie.

Shannon's family was beloved in the area, and her father and brothers had opened several thriving businesses. She was a successful entrepreneur in her own right, and she had the libertarian mindset to match. She and Ryan seemed, by all accounts, to be a loving couple who had stood the test of time, and their children wanted for nothing. In short, she was living the dream.

But it took Caroline all of five minutes to discover that Shannon's picture-perfect life was a fraud. Though they were given everything they asked for, Shannon's children were never satisfied. They were also shockingly cruel and hurtful to their parents and one another, as well as to other kids, and they seemed to lack any empathy whatsoever.

Ryan proved to be as spineless as Shannon had said he was. Caroline had watched as he turned to jello in Shannon's claws, over and over. Her near-constant emasculation of him had made him whiny and resentful. It didn't help that he'd given up his artistic dreams to support Shannon's burgeoning career. Ryan seemed lost in his inner world, unaware of the many affairs Shannon had carried on right under his nose.

First, there was a struggling wage laborer in the Dominican Republic she'd met while on a mission trip. Afterward, she bought him a motorcycle to help him and his wife with their struggling business—and to silence him from telling her husband about their affair.

Shannon also told Caroline all about the sexual prowess of the Iranian PhD student she'd met at a local cafe and had continued to meet up with regularly until he finished his program and his visa ran out.

She cried to Caroline for a week when he left, but it didn't last long. There was always someone waiting in line, someone all too willing to worship her and keep her feeling young—someone invariably younger, darker, and more exotic than Ryan.

With Shannon, Caroline could let loose. The two of them loved making fun of the vapid, shallow moms at the PTO meetings. Shannon introduced Caroline to marijuana for the first time, unlocking a whole new level of artistic depth. Shannon was well-connected in the social circles Caroline was just learning to run in. It helped that she was gorgeous and knew just what to say and when to say it.

Shannon was happy to bring Caroline under her wing if only to say she had befriended one of the unfortunates. In turn, she was grateful for the judgment-free, easy friendship Caroline offered her—such a change from the passive-aggressive approbation of the uptight soccer moms to whom she was accustomed. With Caroline, Shannon had fun, *real fun*, and it was a welcome distraction for them both.

In short, theirs was a mutually beneficial relationship. So Caroline chose to focus on Shannon's better qualities, even when she spoke to Caroline condescendingly and laughed at her political stances. Despite it all, they built an ever-stronger connection, made even stronger by their sons' growing connection to one another.

Chapter 20

When the producers picked up "The Frenzy of Life," neither Caroline nor Hassan could have imagined how successful it would be—the beginning in a string of box office-smashing movies she'd write screenplays for.

The more money she made and the more success she garnered, the less supportive Hassan was. There was suddenly a slew of pressing responsibilities that prevented him from attending her premiers and galas and speaking engagements.

As time wore on, Caroline began to notice the ways Hassan tried to sabotage her work, always coming up with reasons she shouldn't write or generating random problems that needed her attention *right now* when he knew she had a deadline coming up. When she tried to call him out on this odd behavior, he denied it passionately, insisting it was all in her head.

Caroline knew why Hassan wasn't supportive of her work, but she didn't want to accept reality: her husband was wildly insecure and jealous. Because now she wasn't the single mother, dependent on his dime anymore. Now she was a thriving artist with a blossoming career and the bank account to match it.

Except when he was horny, Hassan didn't seem interested in his wife, even when she did show him attention. Caroline eventually discovered why: he had set his sights on easier prey. Like the slim brunette who walked her husky in front of their house, looking in the windows and trying to seem casual about it. Or the fresh-faced young assistant at the mall kiosk who smiled sweetly at Hassan and discreetly attempted to touch his hands when she handed him the receipt.

Far from hiding his indiscretions from her, Hassan *wanted* Caroline to see these things. He wanted to savor the experience of watching her heart break in front of his eyes. He wanted her to break down and apologize for neglecting him by putting her career in front of him.

When she did the exact opposite—directed her attention to the kids and dove even further into her work—it angered him, pushing him to become even less discrete about his actions.

* * *

"He really reminds me of a younger version of myself," Shannon said, laying back on the beach chair and adjusting her sunglasses. "There's got to be more to the story. That's all I'm saying."

"I don't think any story would justify what he's doing," Caroline said, rubbing some more sunscreen on her legs. "He is *married* and he's definitely being unfaithful."

"*Supposedly*," Shannon corrected her.

Caroline rolled her eyes dramatically.

"Look, I'm not *saying* it's okay, not at all. I'm just saying we can't assume. He *obviously* loves you," Shannon said. "Ryan annoys the fuck outta me, but I love him to death, and I've had my fair share of... *indiscretions*."

Caroline sighed and relaxed back into her chair, listening to the sounds of the kids splashing around in the pool. On the one hand, she was glad for a friend who would try to see things in a more balanced way. Most of her other friends were all too eager to encourage her to leave him and be done with it. And at least in this instance, Shannon was right: Caroline didn't *technically* have any proof that he was cheating.

"He's still so *young*," Shannon said, interrupting Caroline's thoughts. "Plus, you guys never had the chance to fully enjoy one another's company without kids, since you already had Audrey."

"He knew what he was signing up for," Caroline said, shooing away a fly that was buzzing around her drink. "He needs to shit or get off the pot."

Shannon threw her head back and laughed. "I swear to God, you Midwesterners have the *oddest* little phrases. *Shit or get off the pot?!*"

"Yeah, it means he needs to either accept the reality of life as a parent and a spouse or he needs to leave."

"Do you *want* him to leave?" Shannon asked Caroline, pulling her sunglasses down her nose to look Caroline in the eyes.

"Of course not," Caroline said, sighing. "But I don't want this either! When he's actually at home, he just whines and moans about bills and about me not paying him enough attention, but when I do set aside time for us, he spends the whole time complaining about bills and how I never pay him enough attention!"

"You really are the man in that relationship," Shannon said, chuckling to herself.

* * *

One day in mid-December, having just completed a writer's retreat—her first as a speaker and not an attendee—Caroline decided to come home early and surprise the kids. But when she arrived home, the house was empty.

She called Hassan a few times, but her calls kept going straight to voicemail. So she texted Audrey, who said she had taken Jamal with her to find an outfit for her piano recital coming up. So at least she knew the kids were safe.

Caroline puttered around the house for a few hours, bored out of her mind and hungry to discuss her experience at the retreat. Shannon had told her that morning that she was also home alone for the day, as Ryan had taken the children to visit his family a few hours away. So Caroline figured Shannon would be happy for the company.

Shannon and Ryan lived on a palatial estate, an hour outside the city. On one end of the property sat their brick, two-story house with a stately wrap-around porch. At the other end, separated from the house by a small pasture, sat an old white barn where Shannon's prized mare and a few goats lived.

When Caroline pulled into Shannon's long driveway, she was shocked to see Hassan's car parked there. Maybe Shannon had called him over to fix something while Ryan was away? But when she rang the doorbell, no one answered. Caroline and Shannon were practically family at this point and they had given one another a key to their home, so Caroline unlocked

CHAPTER 20

the door and let herself in.

"Shannon?" she called as she opened the door. "You asleep? Hassan? Hello?"

No one answered, and a quick look around showed the house was empty. Confused, Caroline pulled her coat back on and walked out through the pasture to the barn.

When she pushed open the squealing door, she was hit with the overpowering, rank combination of horseshit, moldy hay, and fresh semen. As her eyes adjusted to the darkness, she saw Hassan and Shannon, naked and panting post-coitus, in the back of Ryan's old broken-down pickup truck.

Hassan jumped up and began dressing and apologizing to Caroline, but Shannon didn't move. It could have been the light playing tricks on her eyes, but Caroline was *sure* she saw a smile spread across Shannon's face.

Caroline hadn't given Hassan what he wanted that time, either. There was no screaming, no accusations or demands to know why, no tears. Instead, when they arrived home that night, Caroline calmly asked him how long it had been going on and if he'd been using protection.

Hassan swore it was just sex, just empty animal sex. And he'd meant to wear a condom, he really had, but it had all happened *so fast*—over and over, everywhere in town, including in Caroline and Hassan's bed.

Despite the rage and hurt that ate away at her day and night, Caroline decided there would be no divorce. Above all, Caroline Rush-Soliman loved *order*, and divorce was a churning ball of chaos for all involved, most especially the kids.

No, the best response, she reasoned, was the quietest one,

the cleanest one, the one least likely to disrupt their lives. So she made an appointment for STI testing and moved his things into the guest room when he was at work. Then she went right back to working on her new screenplay.

Strong as she seemed on the outside, internally Caroline was churning with rage and anxiety and a deep, *deep* sorrow.

I should have seen it coming, she scolded herself. *I should have known it was coming.*

She beat herself up for months. But she had been blinded by her love of Hassan, and of Shannon, too.

Never again, Caroline decided and built a ten-foot wall around her heart.

* * *

Nothing was lost on Audrey, who immediately took note of the odd goings-on in their house and confronted Caroline, head-on, over breakfast one morning.

"So... Hassan is sleeping in the guest room and you're... unavailable by 11 a.m. most days," she said, gesturing to Caroline's mostly full wine glass. "You gonna just carry on like it's all business as usual?"

Caroline sighed and set her fork down. "Audrey, you're a grown woman, so I'm gonna talk to you like one if you insist on having this conversation. And you may not like what you hear."

"Try me," Audrey replied, taking a bite of her apple.

"Hassan and I... there's some stuff between us that can't be easily worked out. He's wronged me in some pretty unforgivable ways."

"You talking about the whining? Or the jealousy? Or the

CHAPTER 20

cheating on you with several women, including your best friend? Help me out here."

Caroline set her glass down. "I... what? You knew about Shannon?"

Audrey took a bite of bacon. "Yeah. They've been sleeping together for like a year. I thought you knew."

"You thought I *knew* that my husband was sleeping with *my best friend?*"

"Mom, it was pretty obvious," Audrey said, chuckling.

"And you thought I was *okay with it?!*"

"Listen I don't know what kinda weird swinger shit you two get into. That's a topic firmly in the 'none of my business' category."

Caroline sat staring out the window behind Audrey, collecting her thoughts. "Okay then. Yes, it's about the cheating and *no* I didn't know. So we're taking some space from each other."

Audrey looked hard at her mother. "Do you still love him?"

"It's not that simple. It's not about love. We're different people than we were a decade ago."

"People change. I get that," Audrey said. "But seriously, Mom, he went from fun-loving Hassan, who always played soccer with me, to this psycho-religious dude who made you cry and wouldn't let me chill with my guy friends, and now he's this whiny man-child who never spends time with us and mopes around the house when he *is* here. I've got whiplash!"

"Yeah, that's... you're right. It's not normal."

Audrey sighed and took Caroline's hand. "I know you. I know when you're hurting and it's obvious to me and anyone who's paying attention that you're struggling with this. No one would blame you for being irate. But you're acting like everything's fine."

Caroline took a bite of her muffin. "I'm not exactly the model wife, so I don't have a lot of room to complain here."

"Yeah, you're a drunk. We know this. But you're not cheating on him and disappearing for weeks."

"There's more to being a good spouse than *not cheating*," Caroline said. Sure, she'd been faithful, even when she'd had the chance with Rob and others over the years. But she could be vicious and hurtful to Hassan when they argued—especially when she was drunk. She was ashamed of the way she crossed the line with him, over and over, but she couldn't muster an ounce of respect for him sometimes.

"I don't understand why you don't just end it if you're so unhappy," Audrey replied.

"You don't understand because you aren't a mother," Caroline said. "Divorce isn't as simple as all that. It's hard for kids to cope with. I don't wanna do that to your brother."

"So what... you think *this* is easy for him? Watching you and Hassan fight and give each other the cold shoulder and sleep separately? When was the last time you *looked* at Jamal, Mom? He's struggling, too."

"Okay. I have a meeting in a few minutes. Can we talk about this later?" Caroline said, clenching her jaw. The last thing she needed right now was her twenty-year-old daughter criticizing her parenting skills.

"Sure, Mom. We can do that," Audrey said sadly, picking up her book bag and heading to the front door to slip her shoes on. "I'm not trying to tell you what to do with your life. I love you both and I think it might be better for *both* of you to call it quits. That's all I'm saying."

"Thank you. I will take that under advisement," Caroline replied dryly, stepping into her office as Audrey headed out

CHAPTER 20

the front door.

* * *

After her meeting, Caroline opened a bottle of wine, poured herself a glass, and climbed into bed. But before she could take a drink, she burst into tears, remembering what Audrey had said.

It was just like that night when Audrey came home drunk, all over again, only Caroline was drinking *more* than she had been back then. She felt the burn of shame reddening her cheeks.

It had to stop. Something had to give, and she knew it wasn't going to be Hassan. He didn't deserve the energy it would take to either work on the relationship or leave him. So she decided it was high time she sought help again for her drinking problem—if not for her, for Audrey and Jamal.

IV

Part Four

Chapter 21

"What can I get you to drink, Ms. Rush-Soliman?" Stella asked.

"*Caroline*, please," she replied, setting her bags down by the side of the plush turquoise couch. "And ice water will do just fine."

"Yes, ma'am... uh, *Caroline*," Stella replied, blushing, then hustled back to the back room of the cafe. When she returned, she handed Caroline a crystal glass, filled to the brim. "I hope this is okay?"

"Perfect," she said, taking a sip and relishing the sensation as it slid down her throat.

Caroline had been sober for 368 days and nights, and she had the medallions to show for it. It was one of the hardest things she'd ever done, especially when her initial zeal wore off and she had to rely on cold, hard dedication and dogged self-control.

But with support from her AA sponsor and the friends she'd met at the meetings, she'd gotten into therapy and done her best to sit with her pain, like she had that first night. And it was working. Aside from improving her health and her relationships with her children, her writing was better than ever, and she was finally getting the recognition she deserved. She was *proud* of herself for once, and it felt good.

"The podium is ready and Angelo should be here soon to set up the mic," Stella said.

"Oh, a mic? Is that necessary? How many are we anticipating?"

"Two hundred people booked their seats in advance and there are about another fifty lined up in front of the building."

Caroline had entered the bookstore cafe from the alley, so she hadn't noticed the crowd gathering in front. "Well, let's hope we don't disappoint them," she replied, smiling awkwardly.

She still hadn't adjusted to this whole famous writer thing. When her publicist arranged the event, she was hesitant to even accept the offer. The obscene amount of money she deposited into Caroline's account, though, persuaded her.

"Will you be needing a ride home afterward? I'd be happy to arrange one for you," Stella asked. "Or will your husband be here soon?"

"I'm sure someone can get me home," she replied, dodging the question. Though Audrey had a late class at the university and needed the car, she assured Caroline she would do all she could to pick up Jamal and make it on time.

Hassan would *not* be there, she knew, and she was glad of it. They'd been nothing more than roommates for a full year now, and Caroline had given up even telling him about her awards or events. His sour, bitter envy was something she wanted to keep as far away from her as possible, especially at an event like this one.

CHAPTER 21

A man stepped in front of her, offering his hand. "Hello! It's an honor to meet you, Ms. Rush-Soliman! I am *such* a fan!"

"That's very kind of you," she smiled, shaking his hand. "Are you... Angelo?"

"Yep! That's me," he said, pulling out a wireless mic and arranging some tape on the mouthpiece. "I'm just gonna situate this and make sure it's working as it should."

"Yes, thank you," she replied. Once he had the mic positioned and taped down on her cheek, he handed her the battery pack, which she stuffed into her back pocket. After a few minutes of testing the audio and readjusting the mic, he gave her the thumbs up.

A few minutes later, Stella opened the doors and the guests began filing in, milling around to find their seats and grab some refreshments before the event started.

"Mom!" Audrey called out from behind her

"You made it!" she said, hugging Audrey.

"Of course we did, Mama!" Jamal said, beaming up at his mother and waiting his turn for a hug.

"Wouldn't miss it for the world," Audrey said. "Also, I wanted to introduce you to Ky."

"Hello, Ky!" Caroline smiled, embracing them. "I'm so pleased to finally meet you!"

Ky smiled awkwardly. "I've heard so much about you, ma'am. I apologize if it's not the best timing for an introduction, here at your event, I mean."

"Nonsense!" she smiled, gesturing to the three of them to take a seat in the front row. "I hope I won't bore you to tears!"

"If you will all find your seats," Stella said into her mic, "we want to get started. If our special guest could make her way up to the podium?"

"That's my cue!" she said, squeezing Jamal's shoulder and heading up to the stage.

"As you probably already know, our speaker tonight is a screenwriter extraordinaire." The crowd applauded. "She is the winner of the Alliance of Women Film Journalists Award for Best Woman Screenwriter for her work on the popular movie series 'The Frenzy of Life.' Her newest screenplay, 'Singing Roses,' was recently picked up by an independent studio, so we can all look forward to watching Fiona Glass bring the main character to life next summer. Without further ado, allow me to introduce Ms. Caroline Rush-Soliman."

The room erupted in applause as she stepped up to the podium. Above the noise of the crowd, Audrey and Jamal were hooting and hollering loudly.

"Thank you for that generous welcome," Caroline said. "I am truly honored to be here tonight, speaking with you all on the subject of screenwriting. Honored and humbled. Because the truth is, screenwriting isn't something I took to naturally like a duck takes to water. I like to say that writing, for me, is always more like being thrown in the deep end without floaties and hoping for the best." The audience laughed.

For the next hour, Caroline regaled them with stories of the places she had been forced to write—between night feedings with Jamal asleep in his crib next to her, in the back row of a piano recital for Audrey, or on a bus from her house to the local university between jobs.

She also answered their many questions about how to get started writing screenplays, how to pitch them to agents, and how to be patient while their agents searched for a studio willing to pitch their scripts to producers.

By the end, Caroline was pleasantly exhausted and more

than ready to head home. But Audrey had other plans.

"Let's drop Jamal off at home and head out for some shakes," she said, pulling Ky behind her.

* * *

At the diner, Caroline sat across the booth from Audrey and Ky, absentmindedly scribbling on the napkin in front of her as the two of them laughed and flirted.

Caroline got a good look at her daughter. Audrey was more radiant and hopeful than Caroline had ever seen her, and she suspected that Ky had something to do with it.

She had called Caroline a few months after they had met, gushing about Ky—a PhD student in the Economics of Underdeveloped Countries program at UCLA. Somehow every conversation they'd had since then had ultimately circled back around to Ky—what they listened to, where they'd traveled, the deep/funny/crazy thing they'd said the other night.

"I'm glad to finally get the chance to meet you, Ky," Caroline smiled. "Are you from L.A.?"

"No," Ky said, smiling. "I'm a transplant from Ohio."

"Interesting! And how did you end up here?"

"Well, it's *definitely* a story," Ky began.

Audrey stood. "I need to use the bathroom. Be nice, you two!"

"I thought I detected a Midwestern accent!" Caroline smiled at Ky once Audrey walked away. "I love me a good Buckeye. I'm from Indiana, myself."

"Yeah, Audrey told me. We're planning to head that way over Christmas to meet Grandpappy Charlie."

"Oh, he will *love* you, I promise. Anyway, you were telling me how you ended up so far from home?"

"Well," they said, "I spent my gap year traveling, mostly in China. I wanted to learn more about where I came from, since my adoptive parents didn't really know much at all."

"What an incredible experience that must have been!"

"Yeah, it was pretty awesome. Anyway, I met some people during a trip to Tibet and we struck up a conversation about the program they were gonna be starting at UCLA. I just *knew* it was the right path for me, too, so when I got home I packed up my stuff and drove straight here. Found a studio apartment, got a job at a pet shelter, and applied for all the scholarships I could find."

"You do have quite the story! I'm so glad you and Audrey have found one another."

"Me, too," Ky smiled big. "She's kinda one of the best things that's ever happened to me. You've raised a phenomenal person, Caroline."

"Thank you for loving her as she deserves," Caroline replied, taking a long drink of iced water. "It's such a relief knowing she's in good hands."

"She really is," Ky said. They looked nervous for a moment, then dug around in their book bag and pulled out a small, square box. "I know it's only been six months, but I am sure about Audrey—more sure than I've ever been about anything in my life," they said, beaming.

Before Caroline could respond, Audrey came walking back to the table and Ky hurriedly stuffed the ring box back in their bag.

The conversation continued for a bit longer before Caroline found an excuse to head home.

CHAPTER 21

"See you at Christmas! Love you, Mama!" Audrey called to Caroline in the driveway as she drove away.

* * *

When Caroline walked inside, the house was dark, save for a hallway light in the stairwell leading up to her room.

Hassan must have turned in early, she thought as she removed her shoes and coat and began walking up the stairs. But when she turned the corner onto the landing, she stepped right into a pile of rose petals—a path of them leading to her bedroom. Gentle music played in the background while the water was running.

"Welcome home, baby," Hassan said from the bathroom. When she walked in, the room was lit with dozens of candles and the bathtub was full of bubbles, cascading down the side of the tub onto the floor.

"What a surprise!" she said, smiling and sitting on the stool next to her vanity.

"How did it go?" Hassan asked, approaching her from behind and rubbing her shoulders.

"Fine, I guess. I got to spend some time with Audrey and Ky," she said, removing her earrings. "Audrey seems happy with them."

"Yeah, Ky is awesome," Hassan replied.

"Wait, you already met them?"

"Once or twice, no big deal."

"Well, I think it's—" she began, but Hassan turned her around to face him and placed both his hands on the sides of her face. He looked into her eyes and pulled her in for a kiss. It was the first time he'd touched her in months.

Caroline felt conflicted, but when he began undressing her and helped her into the Jacuzzi, her misgivings began to fall away like the rose petals beneath her feet.

"Go on," Hassan said, undressing himself.

"I think Ky's gonna propose to her soon," Caroline said, relaxing in the tub. "They showed me the ring tonight."

"Isn't that a good thing?" Hassan asked as he climbed into the bath and sat in front of her. He'd been working out lately and the paunch he'd developed over the past decade had started to thin. Caroline tried to push from her mind the suspicions she had about who he was working out to impress.

"Love doesn't just *happen* like that, not so quickly. I worry they're rushing into it."

"We hardly have room to talk," Hassan said, laughing. "We didn't exactly take our time."

"True."

"But time will tell, I suppose."

Caroline nodded in agreement, stretching her tired muscles and relaxing deeper into the bathtub.

"I wish I could have been there tonight," Hassan said, changing the subject and rubbing Caroline's feet under the water.

"Yeah?" she asked. *What excuse would he make this time?*

"I needed some time to myself, to decompress after that meeting with corporate."

"I understand." She was too tired to attempt to discern whether he was telling the truth this time.

"And anyway, it was good I was here when Audrey dropped Jamal off. He was exhausted. I made sure he took a shower and then got his clothes ready for school tomorrow before I

CHAPTER 21

tucked him in."

"Thank you."

Hassan smiled. "You look ravishing in this light, wife."

"You don't look too bad yourself, husband," she smiled. It had been *years* since he looked at her like that, and it could have been the high from the event or the roses or the bubble bath, but she felt herself warming up to him.

He came closer and, reaching for the pin that held back her curls, he pulled it out and let her hair drop. "There, that's better," he said, brushing some hair away from her shoulder and kissing her gently there. "Let me show you how proud I am of you tonight. You deserve it."

Hassan savored her like a criminal enjoying his first meal as a free man. He took his time with her, adoring her every inch. When she fell asleep in his arms that night, her hair still damp from the bath, she felt a glimmer of hope for the first time in years.

Chapter 22

Caroline's dress was sticking to her back, and her makeup was sweating down her face.

"Lord it's *hot*," she mumbled to Sharice, who stood next to her, looking cool as a cucumber under the L.A. sun in her neon pink jumper.

"I feel *great*," Sharice said, adjusting her sunglasses. "What time is it supposed to begin?"

"Well, the invitations said three, but half of Ky's family still hasn't arrived, so let's see."

"At least the catering is good," Mimi said, accepting a Mimosa and a Monte Cristo slider from the server who circled the lawn, attending to the guests who milled about outside waiting for the ceremony to begin.

Hassan stumbled over to them, carrying Jamal on his shoulders. He was cackling with joy as Hassan stopped and helped him scramble down to the ground.

"No, don't ruin your suit!" Caroline scolded him.

"Aye aye, Captain Mama!" Jamal said, giggling.

"You'd better be in your spot outside the doors at 2:45 or I'm gonna have to take back that offer of ice cream this afternoon," Mimi said. "And you, too, Mr. Soliman!"

"I'll do my best," Hassan laughed, walking away with Jamal.

The small church stood gleaming white in the summer sun. Ky's family had insisted on a church wedding, and Ky had stumbled across this one by accident one day while on a jog. It had been recently reclaimed and restored by the local Unitarian Universalist community, and they asked for almost nothing to reserve the space. It was kismet.

A car pulled up and several people climbed out, looking frazzled. Caroline recognized Ky's mother, Karen.

"Sorry we're late! It was so hard to find this place!" Karen said, adjusting her pantsuit. "And this guy," she continued, elbowing her husband, "was impossible to wake this morning."

"Jet lag," was all he said.

"We're in *California*, Joe, not Taiwan," she laughed.

"Let's find our seats inside, shall we?" Caroline asked, leading the way.

The vaulted ceilings gave the modest building a sense of grandeur that was inspiring. The supporting beams were wrapped in multi-colored rainbow streamers, and the aisle seats were decorated with metallic bows, wrapped in gossamer. The audience, who was settling into their seats, was brilliantly dressed in bright, festive colors.

Caroline spotted Ky from the corner of her eye and approached them. "So it's the big day! You ready?"

Ky smiled nervously. "I've already received a pep talk from Hassan *and* my father."

"Oh?" Caroline asked, laughing internally at the thought that *Hassan,* of all people, would deign to advise anyone on how to maintain a happy marriage. "What did they say?"

"Well, my dad advised me to always keep Audrey's best interests in mind, especially when she's struggling to see them herself."

"Good advice. And Hassan?"

"Mostly he said I should do my best to provide," Ky said, shifting nervously, "which was... odd."

Caroline sighed. "Yeah... that sounds like him. It's a culture thing."

"But he talked to me like I was *the man of the family* or something."

"You have every right to be upset about that, Ky."

"Yeah, I guess," Ky said, fidgeting with their engagement ring. Audrey had insisted they both wear one when Ky had proposed to her over Spring Break. "I know he cares about us, and he was probably just doing what he thought was best. But I didn't expect that from him."

"Absolutely."

"Anyway," Ky said, taking a deep breath. "I'd better make my way to the front."

"For what it's worth, I know the two of you will be such wonderful partners to one another," Caroline said, hugging him. "You are a *blessing* to our family."

"Thanks," Ky smiled, relaxing.

Caroline found her seat at the front of the church next to Karen, who was busy in conversation with Joe.

As she sat waiting for the ceremony to begin, Caroline's mind drifted back to her own wedding day and the sense of hope she felt, imagining the wide-open future she thought she would share with Hassan by her side. Things hadn't quite gone according to plan, but she'd found a bright future of her own,

CHAPTER 22

nonetheless, and plenty of reasons for joy.

As the music swelled and the doors opened, everyone turned to see the wedding party walking down the aisle toward Ky and their party at the front of the church.

First, there was Pippa, Ky's cousin and close friend, walking arm-in-arm with Clint, Audrey's friend from college. Next, Grandpappy walked alongside one of Ky's sisters. Jamal entered next, walking with his head high alongside Ky's niece, Carissa.

When Caroline looked back at the front of the church, Ky was crying gently, wiping away their tears with the rainbow handkerchief their brother handed them.

Caroline mustered the courage to turn back and look at Audrey. She was walking arm-in-arm with Hassan, shimmering in her glittery, pastel dress. She looked radiant with joy and Caroline could feel Audrey's excitement. But Audrey saw nothing but Ky, her eyes laser-focused as she walked toward them.

For a moment, Caroline's mind drifted to Audrey's father, Paul. What if he'd lived long enough to see this day? Though her heart ached for him, she knew Paul would have been less-than-supportive of Audrey's choice of spouse or lifestyle, so she was grateful for Hassan.

As Audrey and Hassan passed Caroline, Hassan reached out and grazed his hand across Caroline's shoulder. It had been a year since that night he'd made the bubble bath for her, and things had gotten better and better between the two of them. But the hope was still a small, frail flame in her heart that she dared not fan too hotly.

When they arrived at the altar, Hassan hugged Ky tight and then turned and took his seat next to Caroline.

"We are gathered here today to witness the union of these two souls," the minister said. "And what lovely souls they are."

The crowd murmured in agreement.

"What an honor it is to witness the love that has developed between these two people, these two families," the minister continued. "Truly, the power of love can overcome so many differences, cover so many hurts. Audrey and Ky, you have made the decision to unite your lives, to commit to standing by one another through all of life's ups and downs. Are you both here, of your own volition, to seal this agreement?"

"Yes, we are," the two of them said in unison.

"Well, praise all the gods for that!" the minister laughed. "We put so much effort into this party, after all." The crowd laughed.

Ky vowed to cook for Audrey when she was too hare-brained to remember to eat, and to give her all the space she needed when she asked for it. Audrey promised to listen to Ky's crazy ideas and to remind them to take breaks now and then. All in all, their vows were much more personal and sincere than the traditional vows that Caroline and Hassan had recited more than a decade ago.

Caroline looked over at Hassan. Tears were pouring down his cheeks. She took his hand in hers, this man she'd loved for so many years—this man who had happily taken Audrey into his heart and made a place for her there, without a single complaint.

"With the power vested in me by the state of California, I am proud to pronounce you spouses!" the minister said, smiling and wiping her eyes with a handkerchief. "Now kiss!"

As Ky and Audrey walked back up the aisle toward the back of the church, Audrey stopped and embraced her parents, thanking them for their support and love through it all.

"I've never been more proud of you," Caroline said, squeezing Audrey's hand. "You're ten times the person I could have hoped you to become."

"And you raised me, both of you did," Audrey said, pulling Hassan in for a hug. "Now let's party!" she said, wiping mascara from under her eyes.

After the couple had driven away, everyone piled into their cars to follow them to the beach for the reception.

Chapter 23

When they parked the car, the sun was falling behind the ocean, painting the sky a brilliant orange and cotton candy pink. A cool evening breeze was blowing in off the waves, bringing some respite from the heat.

"Being here brings back memories," Hassan said, taking Caroline's hand as they walked toward the beach. "Remember that night?"

"Of course I do," she replied, smiling. How could she have forgotten the night they met, all those years ago, and walked along that same beach until dawn?

"We're gonna have to sneak away for some privacy later," Hassan whispered into her ear, causing the baby hairs on her neck to stand.

"Oh, lucky me!" she replied, kissing his cheek.

"You two are gonna make me throw up," Sharice said from behind them. "And on this dress? That would be a *crime*."

"Mama! Baba!" Jamal called from behind them, breaking away from Mimi, who was caught up in conversation with some of the bridesmaids.

CHAPTER 23

"Hey, kiddo!" Hassan said, pulling Jamal in for a hug. "You ready to *get down?*"

"*Get down?!* Baba, you are *so old!* Who *says that!?*" Jamal laughed.

Bright tiki torches encircled the dance floor on the beach. A bar was set up on one side of the dance floor with the DJ on the other side. They'd also hired a BBQ food truck that was parked in the parking lot, and a line was already forming.

Caroline and the others made their way to the bar to order their drinks. Just as the bartender handed Caroline her virgin mangonada, the limo pulled up and Ky and Audrey climbed out. Both had changed into beach attire and they were smiling from ear to ear. The sight warmed Caroline's heart.

"Where's the DJ?" Audrey asked. "We gotta get this party *started!*"

"They're still setting up," Hassan answered, taking a sip of his martini and pointing over at the DJ booth. "But your brother doesn't need music, apparently."

Jamal was break dancing on the dance floor to the delight of his Grandpappy and the small crowd that had gathered, which included some wedding guests and other random beach-goers who had stopped to watch.

"He sure doesn't!" Ky laughed, taking a sip of the sparkling grape juice the bartender handed to them.

Once the DJ was all set up and the rest of the guests had arrived, the party was in full swing. The caterers got busy passing out plates of BBQ and all the fixings, and more people lined up to order drinks from the bar.

"Audrey and Ky, get on up here!" Charlie said into the microphone.

Ky and Audrey, who had been engaged in conversation with their guests, stepped up onto the platform next to the DJ stage and took their seats at the table. Several tiki torches glowed behind and around them, casting a warm glow across their faces, which were already bright with joy.

Mimi climbed onto the stage and took the mic from her father. "When Audrey first told me about you, Ky, I thought, 'Let's see how long *this one* will last,'" Mimi said. At this, the crowd chuckled. "But I gotta say: you are *nothing* like the others, and the two of you are a goddamn inspiration for the rest of us lonely souls. I'm proud to call you my niece and theyphew," she finished to applause and laughter from the crowd. "Let's raise our glasses to Ky and Audrey!"

"Cheers!" Ky's father, Joe, called out.

The DJ started the music again, and everyone jumped onto the dance floor.

As the night wore on, the air was filled with the sounds of laughter and waves crashing on the sand, and the delicious smell of BBQ wafting from the food truck.

Hassan grabbed the mic. "It's time to slow things down, *way down*. Let's have everyone clear the stage so the couple can have their first dance."

The opening chords of Judah and the Lion's "Our Love" started playing. The crowd ooh'd and aah'd as Ky and Audrey pulled one another in for a kiss before stepping down to the dance floor.

Caroline turned back toward the DJ and saw that Hassan was standing there, watching Audrey and Ky dancing. He looked like he was about to cry again.

"Dance with me," Caroline said, pulling him in.

CHAPTER 23

"Don't mind if I do," Hassan smiled.

So they danced to the music, right there on the beach, barefoot and happier than they'd been in years.

"I love you, Lina," Hassan said, brushing her hair out of her face and tucking it behind her ear. "I hope you've never doubted that. Despite my behavior…"

"Never," she replied, laying her head on his shoulder and looking up at the stars. Because it was true. She knew Hassan loved her; his infidelities were not about her, they were his desperate, insecure attempts to get her to see him, to return his love. And she'd been unable, for so many reasons, to give him what he needed.

"They're gonna be so happy together," Hassan said, tilting his head toward Audrey and Ky.

"I'm sure they will," Caroline replied.

As they danced, they overheard Jamal laughing with some kids his age on the other side of the platform.

Hassan smiled at his son. "It'll be a nightmare getting that sand out of his hair."

Caroline sighed dramatically. "Ugh. Let's flip a coin?"

Hassan laughed. "Not a chance. I did it last time. It's all you tonight, Mama."

When the song ended and the DJ started up a favorite 90s hip-hop song, the two of them broke away from one another to make conversation with the other guests.

Several hours later, the wind had whipped up, blowing umbrellas across the beach and extinguishing the tiki torches. The DJ was taking down his equipment as the bartender made the last call and people began packing up their beach chairs and heading to their cars.

"Where's Jamal?" Caroline asked Mimi as she hurried past her, carrying a giant blow-up palm tree she'd taken as a memento.

"Probably with Joe and the boys," she yelled back, tripping on a rock in the sand and cursing.

"He's not with Dad?" Caroline asked.

"Nah, he caught a cab an hour ago and headed back to the hotel. Said he was too old for these hooligans."

"Sounds about right. I'll go find Joe," Caroline replied. But there was no need. Suddenly, a blood-curdling scream erupted behind her on the beach.

"Jamal!" Hassan wailed. "My boy! No!"

Caroline dropped everything and ran toward them. A small crowd had gathered around, several of whom were making calls while others stood holding their faces in worry.

"What's happened?!" Caroline asked, pushing her way through the crowd.

There, laying on the wet sand, was her perfect baby, soaked to the bone and non-responsive.

"I thought he was with you!" Caroline shouted at Joe. "How did you let him get away?!"

Joe said nothing, but he reeked of alcohol.

"He must have run off with the older boys. Maybe they dared him to jump in?" Karen said.

But Jamal was swimming before he could ride a bike. None of it made any sense.

"The waves," Sharice said, pointing at the stormy sea. They'd been so busy dancing and celebrating, they hadn't noticed how the winds had picked up. Under the moonlight, green, foamy waves were crashing against the shoreline, rising higher and higher.

CHAPTER 23

"*Habibi* Jamal!" Hassan was screaming between attempts to resuscitate Jamal. "Don't leave me like this! *La howla wa la quwatta illa billah!*"

Caroline began to feel dizzy, like someone had tipped the world upside down and shaken it up like a snow globe. She was aware only of her shaking hands, the spray of the sea, blowing against her face and mixing with her salty tears, her vision fading to black as someone pulled up a chair for her.

"The ambulance is on the way," Ky said, stroking Audrey's back, who was sitting on her knees in the sand, weeping alongside her brother and Hassan.

Five minutes later, the ambulance arrived. Fifteen minutes of desperate attempts later, they pronounced Jamal Hassan Soliman dead.

He was eight years old.

24

Chapter 24

After the funeral, Hassan climbed into his car and drove away. No one could reach him for a week. Just when Caroline was ready to report him missing, she received an email from him.

> *The life has gone out of me. I must go and find it again. With my family in Egypt. -H*

She tried in vain to reach him there, but no one would answer her calls, and all her emails bounced back.

Sharice canceled her flight back to Chicago and insisted on staying with Caroline for weeks. Mimi came to bring her food and clean the house a few times a week. Audrey and Ky stopped by frequently to see if anyone needed anything.

But no matter how hard they worked to care for her, no matter how many people called and texted and stopped by with flowers or sent food, Caroline had never felt more alone in all her life.

No one could reach her at the bottom of the hole she fell

CHAPTER 24

into when Jamal died. No one could pierce the veil of grief and sorrow that hung between her and the world of the living.

* * *

Weeks passed. All around her, life continued on like nothing was amiss. The sun rose and fell, the garbage trucks rolled down the road once a week, and the people with their dogs walked down her road every morning and night.

Her phone continued ringing off the hook. Her agent and publicist sent flowers and gentle nudges to keep working when she could. Mimi and Audrey and Ky kept coming to clean and cook and make sure she was alive.

"My son is dead. My son is dead. My son is dead."

It was a mantra that screamed through Caroline's mind from the moment she opened her eyes each morning to the moment sleep mercifully took her each night.

Her hair fell out in clumps and food turned to dust and ash in her mouth. She slept more than she'd ever slept in her life— deep sleeps punctuated by vivid nightmares of finding Jamal on the beach, always a different age, always covered by the shadow of Hassan desperately trying to bring him back to life, but never taking a breath.

There was still no word from Hassan. And time marched on, into the new year.

Chapter 25

When Caroline could finally climb out of bed, the first thing she did was drink a full bottle of wine. She saw no point in being sober now that Jamal was dead.

When drinking didn't scratch her itch, she began throwing herself headlong into increasingly dangerous situations, just to *feel* something again.

First, there was her yoga instructor, behind the studio in an alley—which royally sucked, because she actually liked that place and it took so long to find a good option so close to home. There was also a dashing young scholar she met at a bar—the one who pulled her hair and called her a filthy whore.

The list went on and on, and in the rare moments when she tried to fight it, it was like a monster lurking behind the paper-thin wall of her self-control. It was only ever a matter of time and alcohol before it happened again. And it always happened again.

Beneath it all, Caroline knew what was happening: she was being tortured by the many-faced god of grief, who poisoned her with sorrow and rage and grief that filled her guts to bursting.

So she drank and fucked and smoked and over-ate and overspent again and again in her attempts to purge the pain, only to come home and find it reclining in a room in her heart the moment she was sober and alone. And then the process would start all over again.

Time seemed to wrap around and around itself in a never-ending loop. She felt powerless to break free of the cycle that twisted back around, again and again, in some sort of in-real-time Samsara she saw no way out of.

So on the night of the anniversary of Jamal's death, Caroline turned her phone off and drove to the beach where she'd last seen her son alive.

* * *

Caroline parked in an empty parking lot and dropped Jamal's blanket into the passenger seat. She'd been sleeping with it, wearing it while she watched mindless TV, sniffing it day and night, hoping against logic that it would keep smelling like him.

As she walked along the beach, the wind whipped her hair all over her face, getting it caught in her mouth and sticking to the tears streaming down her cheeks.

Caroline approached the shoreline, watching as the waves crashed hard against the sand—just as it had that dreadful night a year ago.

There was a torrent of rage boiling in her chest. "You want to kill someone, HUH?! KILL *ME* YOU FUCKING SADIST!"

she cried, furiously grabbing rocks and pelting them into the waves. "COME FIGHT ME!" she screamed into the wind, pumping her fist at the sky.

When lightning did not strike her dead, she ran headlong into the waves and dove underwater, letting the icy needles stab her all over. She swam hard and fast, gasping for air as the salty water poured into her mouth and nose, like so many watery hands dragging her down to the depths.

"HE WAS MY SON!!! YOU TOOK MY SON!" she screamed as she bobbed in the water. "He was *good!* And you *took him from me!*"

And then Caroline gave up and let herself sink beneath the waves. The cold seeped into her bones and made its way deeper into her warm insides. She welcomed the crushing pressure.

But the faces of Audrey and Ky, of Mimi and Sharice and all the people who had kept her alive for months, flashed through her mind. How could she inflict the same senseless suffering on them?

So despite the sorrow and the tantalizing release of death, Caroline scrambled up, up, up, holding her breath and pumping her arms and legs as hard as she could.

When she broke the surface, she looked around and saw that she was *much* further out to sea than she had imagined. The ropes alerting her she'd swam too far were easily 50 feet ahead of her. The waves churned, throwing themselves over her again and again, trying to pull her back down, but she pushed herself forward with all her might.

When she finally made it to the shore, she collapsed on the beach, heaving and vomiting up seawater for what felt like an eternity. Once she had caught her breath, she walked calmly to her car and wrapped herself in Jamal's blanket, climbed into

CHAPTER 25

the driver's seat, closed the door, started the car, and drove home.

V

Part Five

26

Chapter 26

ONE YEAR LATER

The labor and delivery ward at Northwestern Memorial Hospital in Chicago buzzed with activity at 2 a.m. Nurses ran from room to room, expectant fathers paced the hallways making phone calls, and laboring women moaned, hanging onto the railings along the halls when a contraction hit.

Ky's father, Joe, sat in the waiting room, twiddling his thumbs and pestering his wife.

"Labor takes a long time, Joseph," Karen said. "Don't you remember when I gave birth to Ky?"

"It's been more than 25 years, Karen! I thought maybe technology had advanced since then, I dunno."

Karen rolled her eyes, annoyed.

"I'll go back up now and check on her progress," Caroline said, walking toward the elevator.

***

A few months after Caroline fought with the waves, Audrey called her on video from their new apartment in Chicago.

"It looks like the family is expanding," Ky said, holding up the black and white sonogram photo.

"What excellent news!" Caroline cried. "When are you due?"

"June 2nd," Audrey replied, wiping tears from the corners of her eyes. "The universe is funny, huh?"

June 2nd. *Hassan's birthday.* "Yeah, I guess so," Caroline replied. "Have you told him?"

Audrey took a sip of her water, eyeing Ky.

"Yes, we saw him a few days ago and shared the news," they said.

"Oh, I didn't realize he was in town. And you told him *before me?*"

"We didn't mean to, Mom. I swear," Audrey said. "We ran into him when we were having ice cream in Millennium Park. The morning sickness was strong, so I turned around and hurled into a bush. What was I supposed to say?"

Caroline couldn't help but laugh, thinking of the scene. "Anyway, how are you feeling now?" she asked. "Do you feel any movement yet?"

"The morning sickness is getting better, thankfully. And I dunno about movement. There *are* these gas pains but they're *not* gas pains? It's weird."

"Yes. That's called *quickening,*" Caroline replied, smiling. "It's the fetus' first movement. It's a fun sensation. Have you thought about baby names?"

"We want to choose a gender-neutral name for them. Maybe

CHAPTER 26

Parker or Avery<" Ky said.

"Or Charlie," Audrey said, grinning.

"Oh, Audrey!" Caroline cried, smiling. "Your Grandpappy would be thrilled. Imagine! His first great-grandchild, named after him. I vote Charlie."

"Me, too," Audrey said, rubbing her belly.

"Well, let's call him and tell him the news!" Caroline said, adding Charlie to the video call.

* * *

The dinging of the IV drip machine brought Caroline back to the moment. "I'll go get the nurse to change out that bag," she said.

"No, I've got it. I need a walk, anyway," Ky said, smiling. "I'll get you some more ice, babe."

"Yes! You're the best," Audrey said, shifting on the birthing ball she had been bouncing on for several hours.

"I'm so proud of you," Caroline said, squeezing her daughter's hand as another contraction hit. "Charlie will be here soon!"

"I wish Grandpappy was here to meet them," she said, wiping the sweat from her face with the corner of her gown.

"He's still recovering from the hip surgery," Caroline replied. "But as soon as he's feeling well enough for travel, he'll head up this way to meet little Charlie."

A few minutes later, the nurse came in and switched out the IV for a new one, then pulled on some fresh gloves.

"I need to check your cervix, okay honey?" the nurse asked.

"Sure," Audrey said, climbing up onto the bed with Caroline's assistance as Ky returned with the ice. Audrey winced as the nurse checked her cervix.

"Any progress?" Ky asked as the nurse pulled off her gloves.

"Lots! That baby will be here within the hour," she replied.

Someone walked into the room behind Caroline. She saw Audrey's face light up, so she turned to see who it was.

"Audrey *habibti!*" Hassan said, dropping his suitcase and bag on the chair next to the door. "I made it in time!"

"You did!" she cried just as another contraction hit. Audrey reached for Ky, who came around behind her and pressed hard on her lower back. She moaned in pain and gritted her teeth.

"It's good to see you, Caroline," Hassan said awkwardly.

"Yes," was all she could muster in response.

Hassan looked down at his shoes and brushed his hair behind his ears. It had grown since she'd last seen him. He'd gained a few pounds, too, and his eyes were sallow, with dark bags hanging beneath them.

"So you're living in Chicago now?" Caroline asked him.

"No. I came into town for the delivery. I'm living with my dad in Kansas City, helping with the business."

"I see."

Audrey was moaning again, this time louder and deeper.

"You feeling the pressure to bear down?" Caroline asked.

"Yes! So much!" Audrey cried, trying to slow down her breathing.

"Okay, I'll go let someone know," Hassan said before heading into the hallway.

When the nurse came in this time, a doctor and a few students followed. "Let's deliver a baby!" the doctor said, pulling on fresh gloves and sitting on a stool at the end of the bed.

CHAPTER 26

A few moments later, another contraction came on and Audrey was breathless with pain. "Mom!" she cried, reaching for Caroline, who stood and held her daughter's hand.

Twenty minutes later, Charlie Journey was born.

Chapter 27

With Audrey and the baby finally asleep, Ky insisted Caroline head back to her hotel for some sleep. She'd been awake for 26 hours by that point and was sleeping on her feet, so she agreed it was probably best.

The morning sun peaked from behind the hospital building, blinding Caroline as she climbed into the car.

"Wait," Hassan said, running toward her. "Let's grab breakfast?"

"I'm exhausted, Hassan—" she began.

"Just a quick breakfast," he said, raising his hands to indicate his innocence.

Caroline clicked her seat-belt, put the keys in the ignition, and sighed. "Get in."

As she drove around, looking for parking, Hassan sat next to her, smoking a cigarette.

"Finally picked up the habit?" Caroline asked.

"We all have our crutches," he replied. "I hear you've been managing your own quite well."

"Fair point. Where should we eat?"

CHAPTER 27

"I know a place," he said, directing her.

Ten minutes later, they walked into a Lebanese cafe.

"I love this place," Hassan said when they found a booth.

"It's certainly unique," Caroline said, taking a seat and admiring the cedar wood all along the walls.

The server approached, and Hassan spoke with him in Arabic.

After he brought their drinks out a few moments later, Caroline and Hassan sat in silence for some time, the two of them sipping their drinks and admiring the sunrise over the city.

"I'm just so proud of her," Hassan said, interrupting Caroline's thoughts.

"Yes. They're going to be wonderful parents, I think," she replied.

"Let's hope so. Audrey had good parenting, but I wonder about Ky."

"Oh? What makes you say so? Joe and Karen seem like loving parents."

Hassan took another sip of his Turkish coffee. "Nothing. I... I love Ky, I do, but how well could they have raised them if they turned out like *that*."

Caroline sighed and stood. "I need to use the restroom," she lied, heading to the back of the restaurant. For all his progressive views, Hassan still had more than a hint of his conservative upbringing to deconstruct.

When she came back to the table, it was spread with all the fixings: *labna*, hummus with olive oil and pine nuts, warm crusty pita bread, runny *shakshouka* eggs, falafel, and fried eggplant. It smelled *divine*.

"Feeling better?" Hassan asked as he stuffed some food into his mouth, dripping hummus on his scraggy beard. He had *really* let himself go. But then, grief had broken Caroline apart in other less visible ways, so she tried to muster some compassion for him.

"No, but I will once I get some of this food into my stomach," she replied, taking her seat in the booth. "And another thing," she began. She knew better, but couldn't stop herself. "Ky has turned out *phenomenally*. They are kind, intelligent, and compassionate. They love Audrey and Charlie. Ky is one of the best things that's ever happened to this family."

Hassan sat speechless, sipping his Turkish coffee.

"What, you have nothing to say?"

"Let's agree that we love Ky and Ky loves her and the baby, and leave it at that," he said.

There was no point in arguing with him. *Not my circus, not my monkey anymore*, she thought to herself.

"How have you been, Lina?" Hassan asked.

She took a deep breath. "As well as one could expect, I imagine."

Hassan nodded in understanding. "What are you doing these days? Still writing?"

"Yes. I recently sold a screenplay to Warner Brothers."

"Ooh!" Hassan exclaimed. "My wife, the *artist*."

"Ex-wife," she corrected him.

Hassan frowned. "*Technically*, you're wrong."

"You abandoned me. That was the end of our marriage, as far as I'm concerned."

Hassan sighed and wiped his hands and face with his napkin. "Well, not in the eyes of the state of California. And anyway, I invited you here to talk about the future, not the past."

CHAPTER 27

"Ah yes, your favorite method of escaping accountability: let's just act like it never happened," she said, annoyed. "But yes, let's talk about the future. What did you have in mind?"

"I've been in contact with an attorney in Kansas City who says we're entitled to compensation in Jamal's death."

Jamal's death, he said. Like he was talking about a movie he saw last night.

"You're a real fucking piece of work, Hassan," Caroline huffed. "The first time you mention our son, *our dead son*, is to tell me you've found a way to capitalize on his death."

"Lina, listen—" he began.

"Don't call me that," Caroline said, putting her hand up to stop him. "Not now."

Hassan dropped his head. "I'm as broken as you are, okay? But... his death could have been prevented, and—"

"How?!" she interrupted him. "Tell me how *you* think anyone could have prevented his death?"

Hassan took a deep breath. "That beach where we held the reception was private. There were no signs posted about the lack of a lifeguard, so technically they can be held liable."

Caroline gritted her teeth in frustration. "Hassan, it was *nighttime*. There was no need for a sign! It was obvious no one was there watching for drowning swimmers. He *shouldn't have been left alone!*"

"I did not leave him alone."

Caroline took a deep breath. "No. You didn't. And neither did I. We trusted him to Joe and the boys. Neither of us is at fault here. And we can't very well sue Joe for neglecting our son. He's Audrey's father-in-law, Charlie Journey's grandfather. That's hardly in anyone's best interest."

"No one is suggesting we sue Joe. I'm saying the owners of

the beach—"

"Go ahead with it if you think it's worth the money," Caroline said, folding her arms. "But I'm not interested."

"That's the thing. We both need to sign the paperwork, as his parents. The attorney says we could get more money if we both filed."

Caroline sat looking out the window and thinking for a long time. All she wanted was to move on with her life, to cherish her son's memory in her mind. But now this man, this ghost, had showed up and disrupted the tiny semblance of peace she'd worked so hard to achieve.

"At this point, I don't know why I'm surprised by you, Hassan," she said after some time. "You thought *now* was the time to show up and drag us all through this. *For money?*"

"Caroline—"

"No. You *disappeared* for nearly two years without so much as a phone call. You left me alone in that house with all his toys and clothes. Every day, countless times a day, I had to pass by his bedroom, knowing he would *never* come back, Hassan. You *left*, like a fucking coward. You just picked up and moved on with your life, and…" she said, running out of words and bursting into tears.

Hassan called the server over and paid the tab. Afterward, he led Caroline outside and helped her into her car, climbed into the driver's seat, and drove to her hotel.

At the hotel, Caroline opened the door and let him in behind her. When Hassan approached her, she held her arm out to stop him from coming closer.

"What are you doing?" she asked.

"Please, Lina. Please forgive me," Hassan said, with tears in his eyes. "I *was* a coward. I couldn't handle the pain. I couldn't watch you crumble like that. So I ran. I got busy and I told myself I was doing you a favor by staying away."

"Hassan—"

"I mean it. I should have stayed with you, with you *both*."

"Yes, you should have," she said.

"I'm here now," he said, pulling her near him. He smelled of aftershave and airplane and Turkish coffee and smoke—like *Hassan*.

Against her better judgment, she collapsed against his chest, crying gently at first and then harder. She gave herself over to him.

The next morning, Hassan caught his plane back to Kansas City. Caroline tried to call him a few times over the next few weeks, and her call was always sent to voicemail.

Months passed without a word. Again.

When he showed up in L.A. six months later to tell her he'd filed the lawsuit against the owners of the beach, she didn't resist him.

Without so much as a question where he had been or why he'd ignored her calls, she invited the sweet release of little death in his arms.

That time, she didn't try to reach him afterward.

* * *

For two years, this pattern continued. Two years of meeting up in random hotels and Airbnbs around the world—a drunken two-week excursion to Greece, a holiday in Jamaica, a weekend in Vegas she could hardly recall. And no one but them knew it was happening, not even Sharice, who knew about all of Caroline's darkest secrets.

There was never a question of where things were going, never any expectation that things would repair between them. They came and went from each other's lives, like ships passing in the night.

Being with Hassan was euphoric, every time. It was a flash of bright, warm light in the otherwise drab, hollow pit she inhabited inside, a delirious escape from the darkness. But the moment he was gone and she was sober again, she was forced to assess the ongoing hurt she was inflicting on herself by letting him have access to her after all he'd done.

When he showed up unannounced one day and handed her a check for $500,000—her half of the lawsuit she never wanted him to file in the first place—she invited him in and let him bend her over the arm of the couch and take her.

The moment he left, she blocked his number, hired a divorce attorney, and put the house up for sale, thanking God she'd bought it in her own name with her own money. Once the house sold, she looked up the number for Mr. Harrison in Wind Point, Wisconsin.

28

Chapter 28

"This place hasn't changed a bit!" Sharice exclaimed when she stepped into the living room. "Wow."

"Give me time, Shar. Just give me some time," Caroline said. She'd already hired an architect to help her plan the new, open floor layout, as well as a designer to help her modernize the cabin without destroying its charm.

In the meantime, though, she needed to toss out some of the older furniture and make room for her own, which was sitting in the moving truck outside.

"The younger Mr. Harrison give you much trouble?" Sharice asked, pouring herself a glass of water from the filtered pitcher in the fridge. "I imagine he wasn't too happy to part with his father's cabin."

Caroline chuckled. "Actually, he seemed thrilled to hear from me."

"I'm sure he was," Sharice said, eyebrows insinuating.

"No, it was nothing like that," Caroline said, laughing. "He doesn't even live in town anymore. When his dad died, he took the life insurance check and bought himself a nice place in Miami or somewhere."

"*Wooowwweee,*" Sharice declared. "Selling his daddy's ancestral home before he's cold in his grave? You sure he didn't have anything to do with the death?"

Caroline laughed out loud. "You're not right in the head, Sharice. Not right at all."

"I'm just *saying*. Not even a month! He couldn't wait *a month*? It's just disrespectful."

They spent the rest of the evening tossing out old, broken furniture and moving Caroline's things in.

Caroline found a painting in the back of the closet in the guest bedroom. A woman, wearing little more than a thin robe, stood in the forefront with her back to the viewer. She was looking out on a mountain scene as the sun set, throwing light around her silhouette.

"You're gonna keep *that?*" Sharice laughed.

"I dunno. It speaks to me," Caroline said, hanging it on the wall of the guest room, which was going to be her office. With windows facing southwest, it had more light than any other room in the house.

"Well, to each her own, I guess," Sharice said, walking back into the kitchen to continue scrubbing the back-splash.

A few hours later, they collapsed on Caroline's couch in front of the fireplace as big, fluffy snowflakes fell outside.

"It's so beautiful here," Sharice remarked. "Though..."

"Though?"

"Well... there's something I just don't understand."

"Go on," Caroline said.

"Why on *earth* would you buy a cabin *next to a lake*? I thought

CHAPTER 28

you'd run as far as possible in the opposite direction of any body of water! I dunno, like buy an adobe house in the desert or something. *I* would have, given everything that's happened..."

Caroline took a deep breath. "I can see why you'd think that. But I guess it's... well, it's kinda like that guy in F. Scott Fitzgerald's short story "Babylon Revisited." You know, the recovering alcoholic who hangs out at his old favorite bar and allows himself just one drink a day. Like... to prove to himself he can fight it, to sort of rob the alcohol of its power over him."

"Caroline, what the hell? As a recovering alcoholic, surely you can see that's a *terrible* idea! You came here to *torture yourself* to prove... what? That you could handle it? There's nothing noble about surviving daily turmoil that you brought on yourself."

Caroline tossed her hands in the air. "Maybe I came here because the waves make me feel closer to him in a way? I don't know. Or because I don't want to be controlled by that fear. Or maybe it's because this cabin is the last place I ever felt at peace," she said, her voice cracking with emotion.

Sharice frowned, feeling guilty. "I'm sorry, honey. I didn't mean to upset you."

"You didn't," Caroline lied, clearing her throat.

"I mean it," Sharice said. "It wasn't my place."

Caroline sighed and sat forward on the couch, folding the throw blanket. "It's fine. Let's just drop it. What are we watching?"

"Your pick," Sharice said. "But if you pick some historical drama, I'm gonna throw this remote at you."

"You are so *mean* to me!" Caroline laughed. "Fine, what do you wanna watch? Another reality TV show?"

"Hey, don't hate on my trash TV habit," she said. "Not all of us have the bandwidth to be swept away to another time and place."

"Bandwidth?! There's a *naked Scotsman* in almost every episode, Sharice."

"Oh oh! Now the truth is revealed. Ms. Serious Writer watches the soft-core lit porn for the kilt-removing action!"

Caroline laughed and stood to pop some popcorn. Her phone started ringing, so she picked it up.

"Hello?" Caroline said.

"Hi, Mom!" Audrey said. "I wanted to make sure you made it safely."

"Hey Audrey and Ky and Charlie!" Sharice yelled from the couch.

"Hi, Auntie Sharice!" Audrey and Ky said in unison.

"You guys having fun?" Ky asked Sharice.

"So much," Sharice replied, deadpan.

"Yeah, I bet!" Ky laughed.

"Mom, can we talk?" Audrey asked, and her voice sounded serious.

Caroline took the call off of speakerphone and stepped into the spare room. "What's up?" she asked.

"It's Hassan. He won't stop calling. He keeps begging me to ask you to call him."

Caroline sighed in exasperation. This was low, even for Hassan. "I'm sorry. I will deal with this. He shouldn't be bothering you."

"He's not bothering me, Mom. I just... Can you at least talk to him?"

"I need some space and he needs to respect that."

"I agree," Ky said from the background. "He needs to stop this."

CHAPTER 28

"I will handle it," Caroline said, pulling out her laptop to write Hassan a strongly worded email. "How is my Charlie?"

"Oh, she's just fine," Audrey replied. "They're watching Frozen."

"I love that movie! Do you need anything for her? I'll be in Chicago next month for that conference. I could bring her some clothes or—"

"Mom, we barely have room for her things as it is," Audrey said.

"Thanks, Mom!" Ky called out in the background.

"Okay, well, I better get back in there and eat some popcorn before Sharice eats it all."

"Alright," Audrey replied. "Stay safe, okay? I heard there's a storm brewing behind you, headed our way in a few days."

"Yeah, it just started snowing. But don't worry. We're not going anywhere until we return the moving truck on Sunday night. We'll be fine."

"Good. Hug Auntie Sharice for me," Audrey said. "Charlie, tell Grandma bye!"

Charlie gurgled something or other into the phone and Caroline overheard Ky and Audrey laughing in the background.

"Yes, that's right! Grandma loves you, too, Charlie! Bye, guys!"

Caroline ended the call and headed back into the living room. The fire was dying down, so she threw another log on the fire and joined Sharice on the couch.

Chapter 29

Caroline awoke the next morning to a knock at the door.

"Mimi!" she smiled when she opened the door, wrapping her arms around her sister. "What are you doing here?!"

"Do I have to have a reason to come visit my big sister in her fancy new house?" Mimi asked, closing the door and shaking the snowflakes out of her long, red hair.

"You'd *better* have a good reason for waking me up before 10 a.m. on a weekend," Sharice said, standing from the couch and stretching. "It's criminal."

"Okay, *fine*, I have a reason. I'll be right back," she said, stepping back out the front door.

Caroline looked at Sharice, eyebrows raised.

"Hey, I know as much as you do," she said, shrugging.

When Mimi stepped back inside, she was carrying a red, plastic kennel. There was a faint whimpering coming from within when she set it down on the ground and removed her coat and boots.

CHAPTER 29

"You got me a puppy?!" Caroline cried.

"Close! I got *me* a puppy, and I brought her to visit her Auntie Caroline," she smiled, unlatching the kennel. Out stepped an adorable Yorkie, who ran into Mimi's waiting arms. "Her name's Tinkerbell!"

"*Tink*," Caroline said, smiling. "Perfect name!"

Sharice walked past her into the kitchen, grabbing a mug and filling it with coffee. "I'm just saying... this coulda been a video call," she said, grumbling. But when Mimi sat Tink down, she ran straight to Sharice. And just like that, her hard exterior melted away.

The three of them spent the day together, taking turns choosing movies and sharing bowls of popcorn and chocolate-covered pretzels—Caroline's favorite.

* * *

That evening, Mimi went to take a shower and came out wearing tight, low-cut jeans and a fitted flannel.

"Where are *you* going?" Caroline asked her.

"Correction: where are *we* going. And the answer: it's a surprise!"

"Mimi..." she began. "It's snowing!"

"Hey, no arguments. I'm an excellent driver! And I brought you a puppy-niece and some chocolate-covered pretzels. Now you're going to entertain me by going out somewhere fun. And Sharice can come, too."

"Don't gotta ask me twice!" Sharice laughed, stepping into the guest room to find some clothes to wear.

"Okay, if you're gonna force me, I suppose..." Caroline said, smiling. Mimi always seemed to know what she needed before she did.

* * *

Caroline stepped out of Mimi's Honda CRV in downtown Racine. Mimi led the way, her silver heels clicking on the snow-laden brick road. When she stopped in front of what looked like a seedy bar, Caroline shook her head.

"Here? You took me out of my cozy cabin and made me wear actual pants—for *this*?!"

"Don't judge a book by its cover, Ms. Big Name Writer," she said, poking Caroline in the shoulder. "This place has the best wings in town, and I hear the company isn't bad either."

"I knew it!" Sharice laughed. "It's all about the menfolk for you, isn't it?"

"We can't all be lucky enough to snatch a hottie like Jayden, Sharice," Mimi laughed.

Sharice stood up taller, dusting her shoulders off. "No, I suppose you can't. Oh well, sucks to suck."

They walked into the bar and found it exactly as Caroline had anticipated: a dark, seedy bar, with the requisite octogenarians at the bar, casino games along the walls, and pool tables in the back.

All that's missing is a hillbilly singing a sad country song, she thought.

Right on cue, a forty-something bald man with forty extra pounds around the middle stepped up to the microphone just as the opening chords of "Tennessee Whiskey" were pouring out of the tinny bar speakers.

CHAPTER 29

Sometimes, the book absolutely matches the cover, Caroline thought.

"Mimi, I dunno. These men are all *easily* as old as dad," she began. "I mean, that's cool if that's your kinda thing—"

"Shh don't think. Just drink. And pick out a karaoke song."

After two glasses of Coke & Rum, Caroline finally got up the courage to sing a glowing rendition of Tracy Chapman's "Fast Car" to the cheers of the crowd.

"Luke!" Mimi squealed as a tall, dark, and handsome stranger approached the bar. "You made it!"

"Of course, *amore*," he smiled, kissing her on both cheeks. "A chance to watch you sing karaoke?! I wouldn't miss it for the world!"

"Luciano, I'd like you to meet my big sister, Caroline Rush-Soliman."

"Rush," Caroline corrected her. "Just Rush." She hadn't *actually* changed her name back yet since the divorce was finalized, but hell, now was as good a time as any to start practicing.

"Well, Ms. Rush," Luciano said, taking her hand and kissing it lightly. "It's a pleasure to meet you, finally."

"Oh no. Has she told you horror stories?" she laughed nervously.

"No, nothing of the sort!" he smiled. "Only good things, I promise."

"Well, we know you *look* good, but can you sing?" Sharice asked him.

"This is my good friend, Sharice," Caroline said, introducing them.

"I love to sing, but I doubt anyone would know the songs I

like to sing," he laughed.

"That's hardly true!" Mimi laughed, handing Luciano a Negroni. "He does a *mean* rendition of 'Friends in Low Places.'"

"Now *that* I *must* see!" Caroline laughed.

"Bartender!" Luciano called out. "Get these ladies whatever they like. I'm gonna need them *much* drunker before I sing."

Caroline took the chance and pulled Mimi aside, making an excuse to use the bathroom.

"Did you *invite some guy you slept with?! And introduce him to me?!*" she whisper-yelled.

Mimi laughed out loud. "Noooo, *of course not*. Luke's an old friend from art school! We are *not* like that. Not at *all*. I invited him as a sort of surprise blind date for you, okay?"

Caroline sighed. "Maybe I don't *want* to meet anyone. Did you think of that? And he's like… 24?!"

Mimi blushed. "You're right. I'm not… listen. Luke is a good guy. He's young, yes, but he's a good guy. Cut loose, ya crazy control freak! Have a little fun!"

"What does he think this is? A booty call?!"

"Only if that's what *you* want it to be," Mimi winked.

So Caroline stepped back into the fray and headed toward the bar. She was gonna need a *lot* more to drink.

Two hours of drinks, endless laughter, and a half-dozen karaoke songs later, Caroline was happy, relaxed, and warm all over.

As Luciano stood behind her "teaching" her how to lose at playing pool, she had to admit she enjoyed the attention. *I've still got it*, she thought to herself.

"I'm gonna call us an Uber!" Mimi called out over the music.

"Yes!" Luciano agreed.

CHAPTER 29

When the Uber pulled up, Luciano climbed into the front seat while Caroline, Sharice, and Mimi piled into the back.

A few minutes later, the Uber pulled over at Luciano's hotel. He handed the driver a few bills to cover their fare.

"Text me when you get home?" he said, leaning against the rear car door.

"Will do!" Mimi replied.

"I was talking to your sister," he smiled, passing Caroline a slip of paper.

"Oooh!" Mimi laughed. "I'll make sure she does! *Ciao!*"

Chapter 30

Warm afternoon light flooded through the solarium windows as soft music played in the background. The servers, dressed to the nines, brought out bottle after bottle of champagne and plates of tiny, sweet pastries.

"You look phenomenal today," Luciano said.

"Me? How about you?! Youth really is wasted on the young."

Luciano laughed. "It's the olive oil. I rub some on my face, morning and night. Keeps the glow up."

"I'm sure that's it," she laughed.

The two of them carried on for what felt like hours, talking about art and travel and their favorite books. Time rushed away from them and before they knew it, it was late afternoon.

"So, Ms. Rush," Luciano said, wiping his mouth and calling the server over for the check. "Have you had enough to eat?"

"I'm positively *stuffed*," Caroline replied, smiling. "This has been wonderful."

"Oh no! You don't mean for it to end?" he said, frowning.

She had some work to catch up on and had planned to sit at

CHAPTER 30

a local coffee shop after their date to do just that. But she was enjoying the conversation. "What did you have in mind?" she asked.

"A little walk through a local gallery, nothing too intense," he said, smiling. "And then I'll send you on your way."

As the two of them wandered through the gallery that afternoon, admiring the art and one another, the sexual energy was palpable.

So when he invited her up to his loft downtown, she forgot all about the work she had to do and followed him up to the penthouse suite. Caroline had found her new muse.

* * *

After that, Caroline saw Luciano every weekend. Eventually, he started showing up in the middle of the week. Her writing could wait.

Hassan had been like the tide—uncontrollable and destructive, but something she could always count on to come and leave and come back again. Luciano was like a calm, still pond that Caroline could dive into at her leisure. And she dove in more and more frequently as the days turned to weeks and the weeks to months.

When Luciano was around, she felt young and alive. They danced in the kitchen as he taught her to cook Sicilian food from recipes his grandmother had brought across the ocean with her fifty years ago. She became accustomed to the pleasure of ending the night wrapped in his arms, in this bed or that one.

"Can I ask you a question?" she asked him one morning as they lay in bed together, scrolling through their social media feeds.

"Of course," he replied, turning to look at her. "What is it?"

"Don't you prefer someone younger? Someone you can have a family with?"

Luciano locked his phone and sat it down on the bedside table. "What makes you ask that question?"

"Luke, you're *incredible*. I don't want you to resent me for making you miss out on having a family of your own. I want you to have a *full life*, and I'm done having children."

"Do you think having children is an *experience* I'm afraid I'll miss out on? Bringing a child into the world is a serious, life-changing decision. I don't think either of us has the time or the energy for that kind of responsibility right now."

Caroline nodded. "But still. I'm nearly twice your age."

"So what, you worry I'm entertaining you for the fun of it, or until I find something better?" he asked, cupping her face in his hand and brushing her messy curls out of her face. "Don't you know yet that I love you?"

Caroline was speechless. "I... well, I guess I didn't know that, no. And I'm not sure I believe it, not this early."

"What will it take to convince you, *amore*? You want a ring, hmm?" he asked, kissing her hand.

"Dear God, no," Caroline said, laughing.

"Okay, but let's be serious. If I want the *experience of having a baby*, there are other ways to do that, other than the traditional method, I mean."

"Oh? Like what? Do you want to start a conversation about opening up the relationship? Because that's *not* where I thought this was going."

CHAPTER 30

Luciano laughed. "You always jump to the worst conclusion! I meant a surrogate, for example, or adoption."

"Oh," she replied. "Well, that's... better, I guess. But still, Luke, I don't want to raise another child! I'm a *grandmother*, for God's sake!" Caroline said.

Luciano sucked the air through his teeth. "That you are," he said flirtatiously, rubbing his hands up and down her thighs. "You're the hottest grandma on the block!"

The two of them burst into laughter and that was the last they spoke of the subject of having children. Whatever Luciano had decided about having his own children, he made it clear he was content to build a life with Caroline—just Caroline.

Before she knew it, Luciano had earned the space he'd begun to take up in her mind, heart, and life. He was careful to honor her need for her own space, careful not to pressure her, and he made her feel safe, respected, and desired—something Hassan hadn't managed for more than three months in their entire marriage.

* * *

The first time Hassan reached out to Caroline after she met Luciano, she ignored the email. The next time, she was late for a meeting with a director, so she answered a call from an unknown number, thinking it was the director's assistant. The minute she heard Hassan's voice, she ended the call and blocked the number. Every few weeks after that, he tried to reach out to her. And over and over again, she rebuffed his advances.

One night, as she and Luciano sat watching a documentary

about the artist Jean-Michel Basquiat, Hassan called again, this time from a number in Egypt. When Caroline stared at the screen, trying to decide if she should answer—maybe it was his family calling to inform her he was dead, which was something she'd like to know—Luciano looked over at her phone.

"Who's calling you from *there*?" he asked. When he saw the look on Caroline's face, he sighed. "When were you going to tell me you were taking calls from your ex-husband?"

Caroline rejected the call and paused the movie. "I haven't answered any of his calls. I haven't said a word to him in years."

"So why won't he just give up?"

Caroline put her face in her hands. "I don't know. I really don't. Except maybe guilt? Or maybe he thinks it's love?"

"Love *does not* do what he did to you, to Audrey," Luciano said, stroking Caroline's hair. "Are you *sure* you don't feel anything for him anymore?"

Caroline sat thinking for a minute, exploring the caverns of her heart and mind, looking for any semblance of love left there. "No," she replied, honestly. "Nothing, aside from pity, really. He's a sad little man who's wholly incapable of giving or receiving love, and it breaks my heart."

Luke sat holding her hand, looking out across the water behind the cabin. "You would tell me if you felt like you needed to talk to him or see him, right? You know we can talk about anything."

"Of course," Caroline said, and she meant it.

But alone with herself, in the bathroom or the shower or driving or washing the dishes, Caroline knew the only thing protecting her from falling back into Hassan was sheer willpower, and she knew how fickle hers could be when she was drunk or alone.

CHAPTER 30

She worried that if she ever let him get a word in edge-wise, he would cast his spell on her again and the life she had worked so hard to build in the wake of his departure would crumble to ash.

So she committed herself to a strict code: no speaking to him, no listening to him, no seeing him, no reading his emails—and no being too alone or too drunk, or alone when she was too drunk. She installed a spam blocker on her phone and even hired a junior assistant to clean out her inbox and set any email coming from an unknown address to spam.

And it worked, for two whole years.

VI

Part Six

Chapter 31

TODAY

Caroline is driving north on Lake Shore Boulevard, away from Hassan's hotel, while smooth jazz plays on the speakers. The sunrise is brilliant, reflecting off the lake like a mural. The crisp morning air rolling through her open windows is invigorating.

As she drives, Caroline Rush knows one thing for sure: *she is sick and tired of her own bullshit*—tired of the insanity of running round and round in circles and coming to the same conclusion and then running back around again.

That morning, when she rolled over and saw Hassan there in the bed next to her, everything in her body was repulsed by the sight of him. Naked, in the cold light of day, nothing about him was alluring—nothing at all. All she wanted was to get as far away from him as possible, and fast.

So that's what she did: she slipped her clothes on, grabbed

her things, and left him there, sleeping. No more goodbyes. No more lies.

As she drives, she feels completely disconnected from him for the first time since they met at Mark's party. She's *alive* in her own skin—alive and in *so much* pain. That's the part no one tells you about what happens when you drop the lies and the crutches that have been propping up the ruins of your old life: *it hurts like hell.*

She knows Hassan won't give up. Not even marrying another woman will make him stop chasing her. It isn't love, but some all-consuming addiction that drives them together again and again.

Not anymore. No matter how many emails he sends, no matter how many times he reaches out to Audrey and Ky and Sharice and Mimi, even if he finds her address and shows up at the cabin—no matter *what*—she is *done.*

The first step is to get sober again. Alcohol is the gateway drug that invariably leads to him. She makes a mental note to attend an AA meeting when she gets home.

Her phone starts ringing, so she glances at the screen, seeing Mimi's name flashing across it. She must be checking in to be sure Caroline survived the night.

She swipes up to answer the call right as a semi-truck plows into her back end, sending her chest smashing into the steering wheel, shattering glass all across the back seats, and snapping something deep inside her spinal column as her head bounces off the airbag.

When her car comes to a stop, slamming into the car in front of her, Caroline watches from above as several people come running up to the car. Everything goes dark, like she's once again falling deep under the waves of a roiling sea.

Chapter 32

Caroline is standing in a ballroom, wearing a glamorous silver dress that cascades down her figure like it was custom made for her body. Various big-name celebrities are approaching her to congratulate her on her body of work. She looks down at her hands and realizes she's older—*much older*.

Hassan is standing next to her, looking every bit as young and gorgeous as he had the day they met. His smile is wide and genuine as he greets the other guests.

The band strikes up a tune, and Hassan extends his hand to her, inviting her to dance. But the tune is off somehow, with minor notes falling where they don't belong in a perfect staccato rhythm.

"Caroline?" Hassan asks, touching her arm. "Honey, do you want some water?" Only it isn't Hassan speaking, but Mimi. And the band isn't playing off-tune—it's the BEEP BEEP BEEP of the IV drip next to her.

"What—" Caroline starts, but before she can get the words out, the memories wash over her. The sunrise, the lake, the breeze, the decision to turn a new page, the crash.

"Oh, thank God you're awake!" Mimi cries, brushing the hair out of her face.

"How long have I been here?" she asks, turning to look around the room.

"Two weeks," Mimi replies. "Do you remember what happened?"

"Like it was yesterday," Caroline says. "And it's all your fault." Mimi looks at her hard, trying to discern if she's being serious. But Caroline can't keep a straight face. A sly smile spreads across her face, giving her away.

"Yeah, well, maybe keep your phone on silent when you drive, huh? You big dummy!" Mimi laughs, her tears mixing with her laughter.

"Where's Audrey and Ky? And Dad? Oh God, I can only imagine how worried they must be."

"They're all downstairs, love, waiting for their turn. We thought it wouldn't be good for you to wake up to all our faces at once."

"Good call. Probably give me a heart attack," Caroline says, "which I'm sure would thrill you since your first attempt to murder me didn't succeed."

"Caroline!" Mimi says, lowering her voice. "They're gonna think you're being serious!"

"It's the pain meds, sweetheart," a stout nurse assures Mimi as she steps into the room and sweeps the curtain closed behind her. "And believe me, we've heard worse."

"Gosh, *really*?" Mimi asks.

"Oh yeah," the nurse chuckles, wrapping a cuff around Caroline's arm to check her blood pressure. "You wouldn't *believe* the family drama that unfolds in a hospital room."

CHAPTER 32

As the nurse works, Caroline looks out the window at the Chicago skyline. The darkness of the night is filled with thousands of lights, illuminating apartments, offices, and the highway. Caroline wonders who the people are in those apartments, in those cars. What sort of lives are they living? What hopes are they desperately keeping alive? Some of them will die tonight, she knows—some of them in a similar accident to her own.

But not her. No, Caroline knows one thing for sure: she's *alive*. She was granted a second chance, and she doesn't intend to waste it.

She winces as pain starts thrumming through her body, starting in the center of her back.

"I'll fix that," the nurse says, removing the cuff and placing her stethoscope back around her neck before walking into the hallway.

Mimi's phone rings, so she pulls it out of her pocket and answers it. "She's awake!" she says excitedly. Caroline hears Audrey squeal with joy. "They want to know if you're ready for company?" Mimi asks Caroline.

"Of course I am," Caroline smiles.

When the nurse comes back with pain meds, Caroline thanks her and relaxes back into the bed as the drugs rush through her veins, hunting for the source of the pain.

"The doctor will be around soon to give you an update," she smiles. "We're glad you're awake, Ms. Rush."

A few minutes later, Audrey comes bursting into the room with Ky on her tail and Dad hobbling behind them, little Charlie Journey pulling him along.

"Gramma Caroline!" Charlie says, running up to the bed. Ky catches her hand just in time to stop her from jumping up onto the hospital bed. They pick her up, leaning over the bed so she can kiss Caroline on the cheek.

"Gramma Caroline doesn't feel good, honey," Audrey says, stroking her daughter's hair when Ky hands her over. "We have to be quiet, okay?"

Charlie nods and shoves her thumb in her mouth.

"How's it going?" Caroline's father asks, rubbing her head.

"I've been better," she says, trying to venture a smile.

"Yeah, that's to be expected," he says, patting her hand.

"Good evening, Ms. Rush," the doctor says, stepping into the hospital room and pushing the curtain closed behind him. "I'm Dr. Kwon. How are we doing today?"

"Well, I'm alive. So that's a start."

"Yes, that *is* a start, the first step on a long journey, I'm afraid."

"Go on."

"Do me a favor first. Can you try to wiggle your toes for me?"

She tries, then tries again. Nothing. "I... I can't feel them."

"Yes," Dr. Kwon says, scrolling some notes on his notepad.

"Am I *paralyzed*?!" she asks, fighting back tears.

Dr. Kwon slips the pen back into his white jacket pocket. "No, I don't believe so, at least not permanently. But you'll have a long road ahead." He pulls an X-ray out of his folder and pops it onto the light board on the wall at the end of her bed. "Right here, between the T-11 and T-12 vertebra. Do you see that fracture?"

She nods silently.

"Your spinal cord was partially severed in the impact of the accident, so you're in what we call *spinal shock*. It can last as long as a few months, or as little as a few weeks."

"Shouldn't it be... improving somewhat?"

CHAPTER 32

"You were asleep, so we couldn't be sure what you could or couldn't feel up to now. But who knows how much healing your body has been doing as you slept?"

"What are her chances of recovery?" Ky asks, one hand on Audrey's shoulder.

"It's hard to tell. We'll have to wait for the swelling to go down, some of that inflammation to abate, before we can assess that. But for now, the most important thing is rest, and plenty of it."

"Yes," Mimi agrees. "I know *the best* occupational therapist. We are going to get you the help you need. Don't worry."

Of course, Mimi knows someone. For neither the first nor the last time in her life, Caroline is grateful that her little sister got the social butterfly gene of the family.

"That's the spirit," Dr. Kwon says. "I'll be back around to check on you in a few days. Remember: lots of rest and keep your spirits up." With that, he smiles, then turns and passes back through the curtain, readjusting it before he leaves the room.

Chapter 33

Caroline sleeps for another week before she can stay awake for more than twenty minutes at a time.

Audrey, Ky, and little Charlie have gone home, taking Caroline's father with them. But Mimi insists on coming to visit her at the hospital every day.

Luciano, too, comes to visit her once a week, bringing flowers and chocolate and romancing the nurses as much as Caroline.

"He loves you, Mom," Audrey says one night after he leaves. "Even though he's like… two years older than me and *that's* weird as hell."

He *does* love her, Caroline realizes, and she loves him, too, whatever that means and whatever it leads to.

"What did you tell him about the accident?" Caroline asks, overcome with worry that Luciano knows about her meeting with Hassan.

"I told him the truth: you were driving home from Chicago, and I didn't know why you'd been there."

Notably, Hassan never comes to visit. He doesn't call,

either—or if he does, no one tells her. Caroline wonders if anyone told him about the accident. So she asks Audrey about it, in a roundabout way.

"No one can reach him," she says, frowning.

Apparently, all he needed to feel comfortable moving forward with his fiancee was one last romp in the sack with Caroline, or that's what she tells herself. She's both relieved and disappointed.

* * *

When she is well enough to practice sitting up, the nurses come and install a bar above her bed for her to hold on to when she needs to sit up. At first, it's excruciating. But after a week or so, the pain abates. Soon, she's even able to endure being lifted into a wheelchair.

Using the wheelchair is exhausting and frustrating in equal measure, mostly because Caroline is accustomed to being in control in every situation, always. But after some practice to build up her upper body strength, she's strong enough to wheel herself around.

Mimi keeps her promise to connect Caroline with the best occupational therapist in the world, or at least one of them.

Laura is a miracle worker with her brilliant, albeit painful, exercises. Three times a week, she comes to Caroline's recovery room and helps her learn to pivot out of bed and stand, first with help and then on her own with a cane.

* * *

One night, alone and unable to sleep, Caroline finds her mind wandering to Jamal's fifth birthday party. Hassan was out of town, of course, but everyone else was there. Mimi had gifted him a trampoline with a net and padding and everything. He was *thrilled* and begged her to put it together.

"You'll break your neck!" Caroline had said, refusing to open the box.

Mimi reminded her that other than a sprained ankle, nothing too bad had happened when they had a trampoline as kids, and they didn't even have a net!

Still, the worry was overpowering, and it took them all months of coordinated efforts, even pulling Audrey, Hassan, and Dad onto their side to double down on the pressure before Caroline finally gave in and let them put it together.

Hassan had insisted on testing the trampoline—for safety reasons, *of course*. And against her better judgment, Caroline had climbed up the little metal ladder and onto the trampoline with him. She had the time of her life, jumping to her heart's content like she was ten years old again.

Now, tears stream down her face as she thinks of how hard she worked to protect her son when he'd be dead from a totally preventable death mere years later.

For the first time since she awoke from the coma, she feels the old familiar urge to drink and to call Hassan, at the same time—and hell, maybe even smoke a cigarette, for good measure. But none of these are possible, for several reasons, so she has to just sit with the pain. And it's *so much pain.*

The pain washes over her in waves, pulling and pushing her this way and that. There is no resistance, no crutch to lean on, no buffer between her and the experience of being dragged, over and over, across the gravely pebbles and bits of sea glass sprinkled across the beach in her mind.

She cries fat, hot tears, snotting all over the blanket and hoping the nurses passing the bedroom don't overhear. As if someone crying in a hospital would shock them.

But after a few minutes, the waves in her heart calm and the sun comes back out. The pain wanes a bit and she takes a deep breath, wipes the tears and snot off her face with the blanket, and pages the nurse.

When the nurse comes into the room, she hands Caroline a warm blanket, then takes her dirty one and tosses it into the laundry bin.

"Crying is thirsty business," she says, bringing Caroline a Styrofoam cup of water, "but it's all part of the process."

Caroline smiles and thanks her. She leans across the bed to the bedside table to grab her laptop. She needs to check her email—there must be *thousands* of unread messages waiting for her response, all marked URGENT—but they can wait.

Tonight, she is gonna watch "Dirty Dancing." Something about watching Patrick Swayze moving his magical hips gives her hope for her own.

* * *

A month later, Caroline is finally ready to go home. Mimi loads her new motorized scooter into the back of her car and drives her home, where Sharice is waiting for her.

"I'm gonna play nurse for a few weeks," Sharice says. "But don't get carried away, now."

"I would *never*," Caroline replies, slyly smiling.

Sharice stays with her for two months. The laughter, warm

soup, and ice cream, and the crying and the endless rounds of "Golden Girls" episodes all work together to heal some wounds within her, deeper even than her slowly healing spine.

The night before Sharice is set to leave, Caroline awakes to a wondrous, awful sensation: a cramp in her left leg, so magnificently painful that it wakes her out of a dead sleep.

She calls out for Sharice, who comes running and switches the light on.

"Look! My leg! I can feel it! It hurts like a son of a bitch, but I can feel it!"

Sharice smiles. "How about this?" she asks, flicking Caroline's right pinky toe harder than necessary. "You feel that?"

"Hey!" Caroline cries out, though she doesn't actually feel anything. Not yet.

"I'll try again tomorrow," Sharice laughs. "Still, it's something to celebrate," she smiles. "I'll get the champagne!"

"Actually," Caroline says, "none for me, please."

Sharice turns back and looks at her seriously. "You sure?" she asks. "That's... new."

"Yes, lots of things are new now."

Chapter 34

A few days after Sharice leaves, Caroline is sitting in her favorite reading chair when someone knocks at the door and rings the doorbell. Caroline grabs her cane and cautiously stands up, leaning against her desk for stability. The person at the door keeps ringing the bell every few seconds.

"I'm coming!" Caroline calls out. "Hold your horses. Damn." If it's the UPS guy again, she's going to have a word with his boss.

Caroline makes it to the front door, unlocks the deadbolt, slides back the chain, and pulls the door open.

There, in a navy blue suit, holding a dozen roses, stands Luciano. "Took you long enough," he says, kissing her on the cheek. He turns to reveal a whole slew of grocery bags on the ground behind him. "I thought you could use some cheering up."

"You thought right," Caroline smiles, pulling him in for a hug. Luciano steps inside and Caroline closes the door behind him.

As he unpacks the groceries, Caroline leans against the door frame, observing him. She feels a sense of safety she hadn't realized she'd been craving.

"You didn't have to do all this," she says.

Luciano looks up, his eyes meeting hers. "I wanted to," he replies simply. "Plus, I thought we could cook something together. You know, like old times."

The mention of 'old times' sends a ripple through Caroline. She remembers the laughter, the shared glances over simmering pots, the playful banter. But those memories belong to a Caroline from another life, one before the accident. Before she betrayed him with Hassan, again.

She pushes the memories away, focusing on the now. "I'd like that," she says.

* * *

After dinner, they cuddle up on the couch in the living room. Luciano asks what she's been writing lately, so Caroline explains the basic plot of her new screenplay. She finds herself drawn into the conversation, for a moment forgetting the cane leaning against her chair, forgetting the betrayal and the lies.

As the evening winds down, though, Caroline feels increasingly guilty. She worries Luciano will somehow find out about what happened with Hassan. She worries he will be even more hurt that she hasn't told him of her own accord. There's a pit of disgust opening within her.

So she takes his hands in hers and does the unthinkable: she tells him all that happened before the accident.

Luciano listens as she tells him the tale, from when she

CHAPTER 34

received the phone call that Saturday morning to when she climbed into her car Monday morning. Caroline worries she's told him too much or too little, but his face is blank as he listens.

Finally, when she has finished her story, Luciano stands from the couch and excuses himself to the bathroom. He's only in there for a few minutes, but they feel like an eternity to Caroline. When he finally returns to the living room, his eyes are bloodshot and red.

"I'm so sorry," Caroline says.

"I understand, *amore*," Luciano says, embracing her. "I need some space to think about all this. Can you allow me that?"

Caroline swallows hard. "Of course," she says. "Take all the time you need."

And with that, Luciano steps out of her cabin.

* * *

A week goes by without a word from Luciano and Caroline begins to worry. Maybe he's decided she isn't worth the trouble. At this point, even *she* wonders if she's worth the trouble.

Finally, he shows up on her doorstep one evening, duffel bag in hand. "I missed you," he says, dropping the bags and opening his arms to her.

Caroline throws herself into his arms, weeping with relief. "I don't deserve you," she says, snuggling into his neck.

"Of course you do," he replies, looking down into her eyes. "You *didn't* deserve what he did to you, and he didn't deserve the love you invested in him."

"I hope you can forgive me," Caroline says, wiping away the tears from her eyes. "I'm so ashamed."

"Yes, my love. I already forgave you. But I need us to commit to this, okay? No more lies, no more secrets. I need you to trust me, and I want you to know I trust you."

It's been years since they met at that seedy bar—years of learning how to navigate the pitfalls of each other's hearts, years of negotiating the complexities of their relationship, different as they are. Caroline can hardly believe her luck in meeting such a good man after so much hardship.

"Are you sure?" she asks. "It's not too late to change your mind."

"Yes, I'm sure," he says. "Now stop trying to convince me otherwise, you crazy woman."

35

Chapter 35

A year after the accident that nearly took her life, Caroline Rush sits at her desk, staring at the computer screen. The summer sun is filtering through the curtains in her office as a robin sings in a tree nearby. The windows are open, letting in the afternoon breeze, which smells earthy and rich, like the lake outside—vibrant with life.

Looking down at the calendar on her desk, she remembers that Audrey and Ky are coming to visit in a few days. Caroline smiles, thinking about how big Charlie Journey is getting. She's so much like Audrey and so unique, all at the same time.

As she looks around the room, Caroline's gaze lands on her favorite photo of Jamal. He's five years old, sitting on a bench in the park gazing intently at a wooly worm that's crawling up his hand.

Today, he would be nearly 20 years old—in college, or perhaps traveling the world. Maybe he would be falling in love, or out of it. His heart would be expanding and breaking and healing again, but it would be *beating*.

The ball of grief in her heart tightens, pulling her inward. It still hurts like hell, but she's finally come to understand that grief is just love dressed up in grave-clothes, and as long as we grieve someone, it's proof we still love them. Caroline knows she will *never* stop loving Jamal, not so long as she draws breath—and maybe even after that, too.

In her free time, when she's not working on a screenplay, Caroline sits for hours, painting on the back deck. She dances in the kitchen with Luciano and gives thanks to all the gods that she gave him a chance that night. She plays with Charlie Journey as often as she can, marveling at the quiet, simple wisdom of a child.

In short, Caroline's life is so full of love and friendship, so chock-full of joy that it feels like she may burst sometimes. She counts herself supremely blessed.

"The End," she types, smiling to herself. This screenplay is her most ambitious yet, and she feels good about it.

* * *

That night, as Luciano sleeps next to her, Caroline cracks open her laptop to check her inbox yet again.

The email she's been waiting for—a letter from her agent regarding the novella she's been working on since she decided to try something new after the accident—sits at the top of the pile.

As she goes to open the email, a new message flashes across the top of the screen.

"I made a terrible mistake," is the subject line, and it's from a new email address with his first initial and last name, plus the

CHAPTER 35

year he was born.

He's not very creative, that Hassan.

Caroline marks the message as spam, blocks his new email address, and closes her laptop without even reading the letter from her agent. It will be there in the morning. She sets her laptop on the bedside table, then snuggles back under the covers and to Luciano, who pulls her closer.

Caroline lies there, listening to the gentle sounds of the waves lapping against the shore and Luciano snoring next to her. She falls asleep smiling, her naked ass spooned by a gloriously hung Italian man, half her age.

Acknowledgments

Writing may be a lonely sport, but none of it would be possible without the support of a team of people cheering from the sidelines.

This book you hold was my first real foray into writing a purely fiction book, one which I began and put down, picked up and put down, over and over, since the winter of 2019. I never would have put pen to paper without the support and guidance of the collection of writers I have had the pleasure of connecting with over the years—namely, Uncle Karl Witsman and Aunt Donna Carlene, M.I.H. McCool, Kaylee Holman, and Megan Pratt, to name a few.

Jenna Wilson, another fellow author and writing partner, has been the sounding board for so many aspects of this book, and I am so grateful for the kind and constructive feedback she's given along the way.

I'd also like to thank my fellow writers who participated in the (first annual?) Writer's Retreat at Allerton Park and Retreat Center in October 2023 (where I spent my 37th birthday). Your camaraderie and insightful thoughts and questions inspired me. I'd especially like to thank Azlan Smith, of the University of Illinois, who led so many of the sessions. His gentle nudges and guidance in the art of connecting with one's inner writer moved me to a deeper understanding of myself and my art.

My partner, SJon, is the real MVP of this book. He made sure

I ate something, drank plenty of water, and spent enough time outside and away from the screen to take care of my mental health. Many a night eating greasy pizza and watching "Game of Thrones" and "Big Bang Theory" kept us sane through the final days of this book's production—memories I will cherish forever.

My long-time friends Nicole, Rachael, and Kaitlin have been there through the whole process, supporting me and reminding me that the universe has a great sense of humor in sending us exactly the people we need to stay humble and kind.

And of course, I am so grateful for my children and their unfailing belief in me. Dayo, Saji, Rumi, and Izzy: You are my *greatest joys*, far more than any book could ever be.

About the Author

Kaighla Rises is a Pushcart Prize-nominated writer, poet, and seeker. Her fantasy novel *Evryn, The Light* was chosen for the 2022 Ampersand Award for Prose. *Things That Shatter*—a memoir about domestic abuse and survival, which she published under the pen name Kaighla Um Dayo—won the 2019 Daybreak Press Award for Best Memoir. She has also published two poetry collections—*Love, Grieve, Repeat* and *wellspring*. Her work has been published in several magazines and anthologies, including Pulse & Echo Literary Magazine and she was the Featured Poet in the 2022 inaugural issue of Hyssop + Laurel Magazine.

Kaighla lives with her family in Central Illinois, where she enjoys hiking, painting, and connecting with other local creatives.

You can connect with me on:
- https://www.kaighlarises.com
- https://www.facebook.com/kaighlariseswriting
- https://www.instagram.com/kaighlarises

Subscribe to my newsletter:
- http://eepurl.com/hvmwCT

Also by Kaighla Rises

Love, Grieve, Repeat: Poems on How Grief is the Soil of Love
In late 2021, Kaighla's mother died of cancer at the age of 52, sending her into a deep abyss of grief. In the coming months, she would burn most of her bridges, give up all her fucks, have to send her children to family, and end up homeless and broken—again. And then she rose up, built a better life for herself, and found new connections and new love.

Love, Grieve, Repeat is a collection of the poetry she wrote during that year as she worked through the pain of losing her mother, and the shocking experience of finally being ready for the sort of love she never imagined she'd find.

Evryn, the Light

On the tiny island of Kenozaria, where women hold power, Evryn Korina—the chief's eldest daughter—is not what her mother hoped she would become. But when a new, formidable enemy threatens her culture and her home, Evryn must choose between staying in her mother's shadow or embracing her latent power. With the help of an unlikely ally and the guidance of her ancestors, she must learn to connect with her intuition and her fellow women to harness her inner strength and save her people.

wellspring

wellspring is a poetic journey following one woman's quest to reconnect with her inner self after the abrupt ending of a marriage she believed would last forever. It's a poetic story of sorrow, searching for love in all the wrong places, and ultimately finding one's own inner source of joy, peace, and purpose.

35 Lessons in 35 Years

https://www.kaighlarises.com/j529o54pg4

Written on the eve of her 35th birthday, this free ebook is a compilation of Kaighla's guiding values, a sort of manifesto of the thirty-five most important lessons she learned in the first thirty-five years of her life.

Things That Shatter

Winner of the 2019 Daybreak Press Book Award for Best Non-fiction Biography/Memoir, *Things That Shatter* is a "superbly written... honest, gritty... page-turner...". It is a memoir of resilience and the power of the human spirit to endure, come what may. It aims to shed light on abuse and healing within the Muslim community and to help women protect themselves from wolves in Sheikh's clothing.

Printed in the USA
CPSIA information can be obtained
at www.ICGtesting.com
CBHW022134240224
4654CB00004B/16